Friedrich Schleiermacher

Christmas Eve

a dialogue on the celebration of Christmas.

Friedrich Schleiermacher

Christmas Eve
a dialogue on the celebration of Christmas.

ISBN/EAN: 9783337383640

Printed in Europe, USA, Canada, Australia, Japan

Cover: Foto ©Andreas Hilbeck / pixelio.de

More available books at **www.hansebooks.com**

CHRISTMAS EVE:

A DIALOGUE ON THE CELEBRATION OF CHRISTMAS.

BY

SCHLEIERMACHER.

𝔉rom t𝔥e 𝔊erman

BY

W. HASTIE, B.D.

EDINBURGH:

T. & T. CLARK, 38 GEORGE STREET

MDCCCXC.

TRANSLATOR'S PREFACE.

———o———

THE Nativity of Christ, as the visible incarnation of the Redeemer, has always been recognised as the distinctive starting-point of the Christian life in time. Around it as a living centre in the stream of history, all Christian experience has turned; and it has thus been accepted in Christendom as dividing the whole life of mankind into its two great periods of the old and the new, the natural and the spiritual, the physical and the regenerated. When the Church was beginning to constitute itself and to realize the full significance of its mission in the world, it could not but attain to a more definite consciousness of its relations to the natural changes and spiritual transitions of the life which it embodied and diffused. The historical development of this consciousness was mainly determined by reference to the cardinal manifestations of the Divine life in its Founder, and the necessity of an orderly spiritualization of the living humanity it absorbed and unfolded. It was thus that the great Festivals of the Christian Church took their rise; and they became spontaneously authenticated by the responsive recognition of the whole Christian community.

It was therefore most natural that the commemoration of the Nativity should take the form it did in the Christian festival of Christmas, and that it should at once assume a primary place both in the ritualistic celebrations of the Church and in the purified affections of the people. Chrysostom already extolled it as 'the most venerable festival of all,' and, by a characteristic metaphor, as 'the *metropolis* of all the Festivals.' In the Western Church it was definitely fixed during the fourth century as a regulating point in the golden circle of the Christian year. The religious mood which it consecrated was one of universal joy, and the relations it represented were of the deepest and most suggestive kind. Having been fixed at the winter solstice, the solar turning-point of the natural year,—'the Birthday of the unconquered Sun,'—it became vividly symbolical of the mystery of the life revolving in nature, and readily receptive of the expressions of the deepest aspiration of the natural Religions. Amid the shortest and darkest days when 'Nature had doff'd her gaudy trim,' it typified the arrest of decay and mortality, and the return of brightness and warmth to renew the whole round of animated existence ; and so it superseded the old Saturnalia of the heathen world, and the Brumalian festival of the

Sun. As a Christian observance it was specially based upon the tenderest and loveliest page in the Gospel History, and on what is most touching and fascinating in human life. Its essential purity, its higher symbolism, and its universal significance, invested it with a charm, a freedom, and a simplicity all its own. It accordingly gave full scope for all that is brightest and most joyous in religious celebration; and it increasingly gathered around it the fairest and gayest forms of art.

The Festival of Christmas has thus come to be celebrated in every clime of the globe, and by all the means of artistic representation and adornment, through the course of the Christian ages. The grandest cathedrals of Christendom have vied with each other in the splendour and elaboration of its celebration. The great host of Christian preachers from Chrysostom in the East and Leo the Great in the West, down to the thousands and thousands who proclaim its message to-day, have poured forth their highest eloquence on this most attractive theme. The tenderest hymn-writers of the mediæval and modern Church, have embodied its feeling of exultation and adoration in undying strains; and the most melodious poets of the reflective Protestant world, have echoed them in mellifluous verse. Music has added the charm of her delicate resources in accompanying carol and chime, and all the varied outflow of quaint and picturesque harmony in tone. The greatest Christian artists have exhausted their skill in visible representations of the Divine Child in the manger, with the worshipping shepherds, and the adoring 'star-led wizards,' and all the simple surroundings of the scene, watched over by 'the spangled host of bright harnessed angels,' and lit up by the irradiation of a new heavenly glory. Even the lower forms of art have asserted the claim to elevate their broad and boisterous hilarity, by making it subservient to the universal joy; and they have been borne with, from the very gentleness of their intent, to the utmost verge of Unreason and Misrule.

But it has been above all by the domestic hearth that the dear delightful festival has showed its subtlest power; and its crowning glory was reached not so truly in high altar service, or in gay representation, as in its consecration of the sweet sanctities of home. Here it mastered and formed the rude life of new races to gentler ways. And from the royal palace and the spacious baronial hall, with the Yule log ablaze on the hearth, and all the robust and tumultuous festivities of the time, crowned by the natural evergreen of the holly and ivy and mystic mistletoe, down to the squalor and bareness of the rustic hovel, and the dim and cold cell in the forest, it shed its humanizing and unifying influence with deepening feeling once a year. It became above all things the children's festival, and it gave a new and diviner significance to the feeble pulsations of infant life. It annually dissolved the bonds of care, and lightened the burden of toil. It softened the hardest hearts, and shed an unwonted blessing on the poor. It renewed broken friendships, and extinguished burning animosities. It lifted woman to her supreme place in the family circle in the reflection of the glory of the Virgin Mother; and it knit age again to youth with the sense of a common undying life. And so the preacher, the poet, the artist, the philanthropist, the romancist, the antiquarian, the novel writer of the hour, and the sweet genius of the domestic hearth, have all contributed of their best to beautify, perpetuate, and glorify the Festival of Christmas.

But the everlasting theme of the spiritual renovation of the life of humanity, as represented and symbolized by the Festival of the Nativity, was never touched with a finer or defter hand than by Schleiermacher, the greatest theologian of the nineteenth century, who found in brooding over its spiritual suggestions the central thought which was to determine the power of his own system, and to give new life and purpose to a higher reflection in Christendom. His 'Dialogue on the celebration of Christmas' is one of the most characteristic products of his genius, and it has an enduring value, not only from its relation to the great theologian himself, but from its bearing upon the living currents of Christian thought. Apart from his earliest sermons, it was the first literary production which he published with his name; and it is significant that it gave the first expression to the central idea of his new Christian faith. In his anonymous 'Discourses on Religion,' which appeared in 1799, he had opened again the overgrown and choked-up fountain of the original religious feeling in humanity; and with beneficent originality he had made its sweet and fertilizing water flow into the parched domain of theology. In his 'Monologues,' published in 1800, as a greeting and gift to the new century, he realized the strength and significance of human individuality, and spoke forth in ardent prophetic glow the watchword of the new moral freedom. But it was in this Christmas Dialogue that he first attained to clear insight into the vitality and power of the Christian regeneration, and its supreme significance for the whole life of mankind. He had passed through all the terrible struggle of the perplexed soul when the traditional creed upon which it has been resting, gives way; and he, too, had wrestled in his Gethsemane sweat of spiritual agony, amid the darkness and loneliness of unspeakable doubt and despair. Then it was, when shaken from his self-confidence and pride by a humbling sense of common human frailty and error, that the bright star of the East rose clear upon his view, and led him with all his weight of philosophic learning and wisdom, like the sages of old, to the manger at Bethlehem. And here in the vision of the Virgin Mother and the Infant Christ he found the end of all his search and longing, a new and higher view of the Divine idea there finally exhibited to the world, and a sure sense of spiritual peace and certainty which was never to leave him again.

It is not necessary to pause over the literary or artistic merit of this 'precious jewel' of our modern theological literature, as it has been called. Much has been written by way of criticism and adulation upon it; and it has received the sincerest flattery in various attempts to imitate it and to supersede it. It may suffice in this formal relation to refer to the exposition and summary reproduced in the Appendix to the translation, giving the view of one of the most critical and cultured recent representatives of the advanced wing of Schleiermacher's School, and it may be taken either as an introduction to the perusal of this little work of the master, or as a recapitulation of it, according to the taste or need of the reader.[1] Schleiermacher's Dialogue has been aptly called a Christian 'Symposion' in the manner of the Platonic Dialogues, and the student of Plato will

---

[1] The reader may also be referred to Dr. Lichtenberger's excellent summary of the Dialogue, as well as to his admirable exposition of the whole Theology of Schleiermacher, in his *History of German Theology in the Nineteenth Century* (T. & T. Clark, 1889).

readily appreciate the reference.   Brief and popular
though it be, it is not to be taken as a mere pastime
for an unoccupied hour, nor will it give up its essential meaning to the frivolous soul.   Its relevancy and
subtlety, even through a certain bewildering variety and
playfulness, cannot escape the most cursory reader ; nor
will it be denied its right to a special place high over all
the accumulating masses of trivial and irrelevant Christmas
literature.   Its light and airy grace, its natural simplicity
and refinement, its sympathetic and tender individuality,
its catholic comprehensiveness and breadth, its elevating
·points of view, and its deep spiritual insight, cannot
fail to find and satisfy the earnest hearts that are at once
lightened and brightened by the proper mood of the
Christmas-tide.   A more genuine Christmas book was
never written; for no Christmas book has ever dealt
more directly, or more thoughtfully, with the essential
theme of the Festival.   And its sweet blending of high
thought and social feeling, of science and religion, philo-
sophy and poetry, insight and joy, make it not unworthy
of its subject or of the genius of its author.

A genuine Christmas book unquestionably it is ; but it
is more, for it is an interesting and enduring contribution
to Christian theology.   The student of Christian life and
thought will find in it original points of view which
have not yet been exhausted, and which were perhaps

never more significant than now. Without entering
upon these in detail, or blunting the edge of anticipation,
it may be premised that the various standpoints of
the living Schools of Theology will here be found
strikingly exhibited in distinctive contrast, and yet in
sympathetic union. The standpoints of our contem-
porary critical rationalism, of the new spiritual theology
(which is indeed only the highest form of natural
theology), of lofty speculative thinking, and of quiet
mystic feeling, are here presented in their varied aspects,
and in their relative significance for the living tasks of
Christian theology. They are brought with deep thoughtfulness into relation with the subject of the Christmas
Festival, which is shown to involve the cardinal point in
the interest of modern theology. And in dealing with this
delicate and difficult theme, the genius of the profound
theologian leads to the most suggestive and pregnant
results. In his human and ideal apprehension, the unreal
asceticism of the East and the crass naturalism of the
West, are spiritually overcome; and the true and eternal
idea of the Christian redemption is significantly, if not
yet completely, set forth in the light of the modern time.

It is this which the Church above all things needs at
the present hour. Her chief necessity is to find a way
out of the lower entanglements and conflicts of carnal
and worldly relationships into the higher catholicity and

freedom of the Ideal, while losing no hold upon reality, but rather securing it by a stronger and firmer grasp. Of all the sons of men who have given themselves to solving this task during the past hundred years, no one has succeeded so largely, through the leading of the spirit and the ideas delineated here, as Schleiermacher; and the leaders of our own theology have only become leaders in his train.

It is also this illumination and guidance which the world mainly wants, and is craving for at the present hour. Amid the deepening darkness of the natural life . and the intensified struggle for existence, the overcast horizon, and the new social problems and difficulties of the day, it is religion that must come once more to deliver and save the worn heart of humanity. And here, if anywhere, is to be found again the gleaming of the ancient joy, and a new herald voice proclaiming, in view of all the sadness and sorrow of the time: 'Glory to God in the highest, and on earth peace, goodwill toward men.'

And in this feeling we welcome again the Christmas-tide, and keep the old celebration, not as 'an ancient form, through which the spirit breathes no more,' but with the very freshness and sincerity of the prime. The celebration has now become coextensive with Christendom, and all misunderstanding is at an end. For the great theologian has shown us in the Christ as the Divine ideal of humanity, that the glory of the Nativity is essentially involved in all human birth, and is consciously diffused by the higher Birth over all ; and that all human life has thus become sacred and divine. Let his cheerful yet solemn voice, then, be heard, along with all besides, bidding us celebrate the mystery of this higher life joyfully and freely, yet without the profaning presence of an unhallowed thought, and recognise it in its harmony with all the wonders of love and science. And so let ' the merry, merry bells of Yule ' chime once more as they ring in ' the Christ that is to be,' in response to the heavenly chorus over ' the good tidings of great joy,' the birth of ' a Saviour which is Christ the Lord.' Amid all suffering and wrong, all burdens of toil and care, the shortening day of life and the dark and fateful ministrations of death, let the old faith live anew and rejoice in the ideal vision of the Redeemer. The eternal Love once more hallows and gladdens the passing night by its own supreme gift; and the one stedfast star amid the universal change and whirl of things, points brightly beyond it to the happier morn.

> Rise, happy morn, rise, holy morn,
> Draw forth the cheerful day from night :
> O Father, touch the East, and light
> The light that shone when Hope was born.

W. H.

EDINBURGH, *December* 1889.

CHRISTMAS EVE.

—o—

THE pleasant drawing-room was gaily decorated; all the windows of the house had contributed their flowers to it, but the curtains were not let down, that the gleaming in of the snow might recall the season of the year. Engravings and pictures relating to the sacred festival adorned the walls; and a pair of beautiful prints of this kind formed the present of the lady of the house to her husband. A considerable number of lamps, drawn high up and radiating on all sides, shed a festive light around, which yet seemed to play and sport with curiosity; for it showed known things distinctly enough, but what was strange and new could only be distinctly recognised and certainly appreciated after a time and by exact observation. Things had thus been arranged by the cheerful and thoughtful Ernestine in order that the impatience thus excited, half in jest and half in earnest, might be only gradually satisfied, and that the various little gifts might remain surrounded for a while in a glimmering and enlarging light.

Those who formed the intimate circle of friends here gathered together had, in fact, entrusted her with this work in order that she might bring together the gifts which they were bestowing upon each other into groups;

A

and thus what would have appeared insignificant when separated, was capable of being arranged into a stately whole. And this is what she had now done. And just as in a winter garden, between the evergreen shrubs, the little blossoms of the galanthus and of the violet must be sought for under the snow or the protecting covering of the moss, so every one had their own portion hedged in by ivy, myrtles, and amaranths. The most delicate things lay concealed below white napkins or parti-coloured coverings, whereas the larger presents were scattered round about, or had to be searched for below the tables. The initials of their names were worked in little edible inscriptions upon the covers; and each one had then to try to find out the giver of the several gifts.

The company waited in the adjoining room, and their impatience gave a slight sting to the jesting that was meanwhile carried on. Under the pretence of guessing or betraying what would be found, gifts were fancifully suggested, the references of which to little foibles and habits, to merry incidents and ludicrous misunderstandings or accidental embarrassments, were not to be mistaken; and whenever a little stroke of this kind of humour was played off on any one, he did not fail to return it on all sides.

Only little Sophie moved about with great strides absorbed in herself; and her continual restlessness was almost as much in the way of the other members of the company, while they moved about and talked at will with each other, as they were to her. At last Antony, with feigned vexation, asked her whether she would not now willingly give all her presents for a magic mirror which would enable her to have a look at what was hidden by the closed doors.

'At least,' said she, 'I would rather so than you; for you have certainly more calculation about you than curiosity; and you believe, besides, that the rays of your wonderful wisdom are not to be shut out by any walls.' Then she sat down in the darkest corner, and rocked her little head in her upturned hands.

It was not long till Ernestine opened the door, against which she remained standing. But the joyful company, instead of hurrying eagerly, as was to be expected, to the ranged tables, stopped short suddenly when halfway into the room, where the whole scene could be taken in, and all of them turned involuntarily their look upon her. The arrangement of the whole was so beautiful, and it was such a perfect expression of her thought, that unconsciously and involuntarily their feelings and their glances were drawn to her. She stood half in darkness, thinking to enjoy unnoticed the loved forms before her and their light joyfulness; but she it was in whom at first they all found their delight. As if they had already enjoyed everything else there, and as if she had been the giver of it all, they gathered around her. The child clasped her knee and gazed at her with large eyes without smiling, yet with infinite lovingness. Her lady friends embraced her, and Edward kissed her beautiful downcast cheek; and, as was becoming in each case, they all showed her the heartiest love and devotedness. She herself had to give the sign for them to take possession of their gifts.

'If I have arranged things to your satisfaction, my dear friends,' she said, 'see that you don't forget the picture for the frame; and consider that I have only tried to do honour to the festival day and your gladsome love, the tokens of which you entrusted to me. Come then, and let each of you see what has been bestowed upon you; and those who cannot guess rightly, let them bear patiently to be laughed at.'

Of this, indeed, there was no lack. The ladies, both old and young, called out the name of the giver of every gift with great confidence, so that no one could deny it; but the men committed many mistakes; and nothing was more amusing, and also more annoying, than when they ventured upon a witty idea in conjecture, and when it was repudiated and returned under protest as bad change. 'It must just be borne,' said Leonard, 'although it always naturally annoys us that the ladies excel us so much in acuteness in these agreeable little things; for as their gifts betray by their significance the finest attention, far more than is the case with ours, and as we enjoy this beautiful fruit of their talent, we must also accommodate ourselves to this other effect of it, although it puts us somewhat in the shade.'

'You are too complimentary,' replied Frederica; 'it is not so much our talent merely; but, if it may be said, there is a certain want of dexterity in you men that comes not a little to our aid. You like very much the straight ways, as beseems the strong; and your movements, although you do not intend to express anything thereby, are nevertheless as treacherously intelligible as are the gestures of a player at chess who cannot cease touching and trying the doubtful pieces of his opponent, and lifting his own six times over with undecided purpose before he will move.'

'Yes, yes,' interposed Ernest, openly smiling but feigning a sigh, 'it still continues true, as old Solomon says, that God has made man upright, but women have found out many inventions.'

'Then you may have at least the consolation,' said

Caroline, ' that you have not spoiled us by your modern politeness. Perhaps it may be that both qualities are as eternal as they are necessary; and if your honest simplicity is perhaps the condition of our cunning, then comfort yourselves with the fact that on another side our limitedness perhaps bears the same relation to your greater talents.'

Meanwhile the presents were being inspected more closely, and at the same time the distinctively female productions in the way of knitting and fine sewing were examined with artistic judgment and praised by all. Sophie had at first thrown but a cursory glance over her own treasures, and had forthwith moved about here and there curiously inspecting and eagerly praising everything, and above all begging for the nice little fragments of the broken initials of their names. For of sweetmeats of all kinds she was extremely fond, and liked to have great stores of them, especially when she could gather them together in this way. It was only after she had increased her possessions by such a supply that she began to examine her presents more closely, and now she went about again showing off and exulting in every separate article, exhibiting every one of them so far as it was possible, in order thereby to show most certainly the excellence of the gifts.

' But you don't seem to heed the best of them all,' said her mother, calling her attention to it.

' Oh yes, dear mother,' said the child, ' but I have not yet had the heart to touch it; for if it is a book it would be of no use for me to look into it here. I must first shut myself up in my little room that I may enjoy it there. But if any one—for I am certain that it was not you—has played a serious joke upon me by giving me patterns and directions for all kinds of knitting and sewing and other splendid things, then I promise as certainly as I can that I will use it right diligently in the new year, but just now I don't know what to do with it.'

'Badly guessed,' said her father, 'it is not that; for you have not yet deserved to possess such a thing. But neither is it a book with which you would have to betake yourself to your room in order to enjoy it according to its purpose.'

Thereupon she drew it forth with the greatest curiosity at the risk of scattering a large portion of her treasures, and forthwith she exclaimed with a cry, 'Oh, music!' and turning over the leaves she went on, 'Oh, grand music! Oh for a whole life of Christmases! You shall sing with me the most splendid things.' Then she read the names of the compositions, which were mostly religious, and had all reference to the dear festival, the whole of them being excellent pieces, and some of them old and rare. Then she ran straight to her father to cover him with kisses in a passionate burst of gratitude.

Along with the aversion already mentioned to female work, the child had shown a decided talent for music, but a talent as limited in its range as great in its kind. Her faculty, indeed, is not at all limited, as she has a hearty enjoyment of all that is beautiful in every department of this art. For herself, however, she does not readily care to practise anything but what is set in the grand church style. It is rarely to be taken as the sign of a purely joyful mood when she trills half aloud a light merry air; but when she goes to the piano and gives her voice full play, and strikes into a deep tone, she always keeps by that grand kind alone. And she knows, too,

how to do justice to every note. Each tone breaks forth
with a love that hardly tears itself away from the rest;
but then it stands out by itself in measured power till
it, too, again gives place to the next following one as with
a pious kiss. Even when she sings alone for exercise, her
singing indicates as much respect for the other voices as
if they too were likewise really heard; and however deeply
she is often moved, yet no sort of excess ever destroys
the harmony of her tones. One can hardly indicate it
otherwise, even apart from reference to its objects, than
by saying that she sings with devoutness, and awakens
and cherishes every tone with a sort of meek love. Now,
as Christmas is very specially the children's festival, and
as she throws herself wholly into it, no present could
appear to her more delightful than just such a one as
this. She sat for a while absorbed in looking at the
notes, fingered the keys upon the book, and sang into
herself without sound, but with visible movement of the
muscles, and with animated gestures. Then she sprang
up suddenly, but turned half round and said, 'Now
then, leave all your seeing and discussing, and come up-
stairs to me as my guests. I have already lighted everything; tea will also soon be ready, and now is the most
convenient time. As you know and have seen, I was
not allowed to make you any presents, but I have not
been forbidden to invite you to a performance.'

In fact, the condition had been laid down to her that
she would be received among the number of those who
gave presents as soon as she could produce a faultless and
graceful work as a first gift. She had not yet been able
to accomplish this, but she was desirous in some way to
make amends for it. Now, she happened to possess one
of those little artificial toys on which, according to

its original design, the history of the day could be represented by small movable card figures amid suitable surroundings. But this arrangement is usually as good as suppressed by a multitude of unsuitable and even tasteless and burlesque additions, which are introduced to give the simple mechanism as much variety and grotesqueness in its movements as possible. She had tidied up this structure, put it anew into order, with improvements here and there, and it was now set up to as much advantage as possible in her room and lighted. Upon a somewhat large table there was to be seen, in simple guise and free confusion, and interrupted by few episodes, representations of many important facts in the external history of Christianity. Mixed up with one another might be discerned the baptism of Christ, Golgotha, and the hill of the Ascension, the outpouring of the Spirit, the destruction of the Temple, and Christians engaged in battle with the Saracens for the Holy Sepulchre; there was the Pope marching in a solemn procession to St. Peter's, the martyrdom of Huss, and the burning of the Papal Bull by Luther, the baptism of the Saxons, the missionaries in Greenland and among the negroes, a Moravian churchyard, and the Halle Orphanage, which the constructor, as it appeared, had wished specially to bring into prominence as the latest great work of religious zeal and enthusiasm. The little artist had tried to employ fire and water everywhere with particular care, and had made an excellent use of the conflicting elements. Streams actually flowed, and fire burned; and she managed to maintain and to protect the light flame with great dexterity. Among all these prominently appearing objects, the Birth itself was long sought for in vain, for she had managed wisely to conceal the star. It was necessary to follow the angels and the shepherds who were gathered around a fire; then a door opened in the wall of the structure,—the house being only presented as a decoration,—and there in a room, which was properly placed outside, was to be seen the Holy Family. All was dark in the poor hovel; only a strong hidden light irradiated the head of the Child, and formed a reflection upon the bended face of the mother. In contrast to the wild flames on the outside, this mild splendour appeared in comparison really as heavenly light to earthly light. Sophie herself joined in praising this with visible satisfaction as her highest work of art. She seemed to herself in making it like a second Correggio, and made a great mystery of the arrangement. Only she said that as yet she had planned in vain how to bring in a rainbow too; because, she thought, that Christ was the true surety that life and joy will nevermore perish in the world.

She knelt down for some moments before her work, her little head reaching only up to the table, and she gazed intently into the little room. Suddenly she perceived that her mother was standing just behind her, and she turned round without altering her position, and said with deep feeling, 'Oh mother, you might just as well be the happy mother of the divine babe! Are you indeed not sorry that you are not? And is not this the reason why mothers prefer the boys? But think only of the holy women who followed Jesus, and of all that you have told me about them. Certainly I will be such a one, as you now are one.' The mother, with deep emotion, raised her and kissed her.

The rest of them meanwhile severally examined the little details of her work. Antony stood looking on

with particular earnestness. He had his younger brother
beside him, and began to point out and explain all he
knew with the fluent and gushing vanity of a cicerone.
The boy appeared very attentive, yet understood nothing
at all, but always wished at intervals to catch the water
and the flames in order to convince himself that they
were real, and not an illusion.

While most of them were still occupied in this way,
Sophie plied her father softly with a request that he
would come with Frederica and Caroline into the other
room, where the latter sat down at the piano, and they
sang together the hymn, 'Let us love Him,' and the
chorale, 'Welcome to this Vale of Sorrow,' as well as
some other pieces from Reichardt's *Cantilena*, in which
the joy and the feeling of being saved and humble devotion are so beautifully expressed. They soon had the
whole company as devout listeners; and when they had
finished, as always happens, the religious music produced
at first a quiet satisfaction and retirement of soul. There
followed a few silent moments, in which, however, they
all knew that the heart of each of them was lovingly
directed towards the others, and towards something still
higher.

The call to tea soon gathered them again in the
drawing-room. Sophie alone remained for a considerable
time in diligent exercise at the piano, and only came in
haste, and without much interest, among them to quench
her thirst.

The members of the company went up and down,
and busied themselves again with the presents. It was
only now, after something else had occurred, that they
appeared to have come rightly into possession of their
new property, and that the things could therefore now be

regarded by the donors of them as not their own, and could be openly praised. Much had been previously overlooked by several of them ; and in some things certain special excellences were only now discovered.

'This time,' said Ernest, 'we have indeed a specially favourable year for rejoicing in our gifts ; some important changes are at hand. The pretty little clothes with which Agnes has been so richly presented, the nice little jewels for our future relation, my good Frederica, the travelling wraps for Leonard, even the school-books for your Antony, dear Agnes, all these point to progress ; and such happy events bring home to us in a vivid manner at present the joys of the future. And if the festival itself is the proclamation of a new life for the world, it will naturally be most impressive and gladden-ing to us when something new of importance is occurring in our own life. I embrace you anew, my beloved one, as a gift of this day. As if you were just now given to me along with the Redeemer, a wonderful festal feeling of high joy seizes upon me. Yes, it even pains me that all who are here are not like us kneeling devoutly before a new stage of life ; that to you, dear friends, there is nothing great approaching which is immediately associated with the greatest of all objects. And I fear that our gifts must appear but meaningless to you compared with yours to us. Your state of mind may be indeed cheerful and happy, but still it is less moved and exalted, indeed I might even say, it must be indifferent in comparison with ours.'

'Certainly you are very kind,' replied Edward, 'to give a glance over with such sympathy at us from out of your enthusiasm ; but surely this very enthusiasm removes us much too far away from you. Only consider that our calm happiness is just the same as that which you are approaching, and that every genuine enthusiasm, including that of love, never grows old, but is always capable of being renewed. Or is it possible that you regard Ernestine's feeling at the expression of childish devotion and deep piety in our Sophie as indifference; or can you think of all this as being without the liveliest activity of the fancy, yet as having the present, the past, and the future entwined in it? Only see how deeply she is moved, as if she were bathing in a sea of the purest happiness.'

'Yes, I readily confess it,' said Ernestine. 'She has transported me with joy just now by her few words. But I do her wrong; these words by themselves may rather have appeared as affectation to one who does not know her. It was the whole view of the child taken all together that moved me. The angelic purity of her heart seemed to open up so gloriously; and if you understand what I mean, as I cannot otherwise express it, in her great simplicity and unconsciousness there was such deep underlying intelligence of feeling, that I was overwhelmed by a presentiment of the fulness of the beauty and amiability which must necessarily grow forth out of it. Truly I feel that in one respect she did not say too much when she said that I might well be also the mother of the adorable child, because I can with true meekness reverence in my daughter, as Mary in her Son, the pure revelation of the divine, without the right relation of mother and child becoming thereby in the least disturbed.'

'We are all quite agreed on this point,' said Agnes, 'that the so-called fondling and spoiling which springs, not from a love to the children, but only to oneself, in order to be spared what is disagreeable, can have nothing to do with what you mean.'

'We women understand that well,' replied Ernestine, 'but it is a question whether it ought not to be sometimes expressly laid to the charge of you men when your special care, especially for the boys, is in question. With them boldness and cleverness are required, and progress is always connected with effort and denial; and so it may often be necessary to keep down the magnifying influence of the feeling of self; and this might easily give their fathers an incorrect view of things if they were not to be diligently guided by our motherly doing and sense.'

'True, we know and recognise,' said Edward, 'how you are destined and made to cherish and develop the first pure germs of childhood, before any corruption appears or attaches itself. The women who devote themselves to this holy service would everywhere becomingly dwell in the interior of the temple as vestals who watch the sacred fire. We, on the contrary, must move out and march forth in stern form; we must practise discipline and preach repentance, or lay the cross upon us as pilgrims, and gird us with the sword, in order to seek a lost sanctuary and win it again.'

'You take me back again,' broke in Leonard, 'to a thought which I had almost lost sight of in the flow of your conversation. It refers to your Sophie, and it has been often of late almost on my tongue, and has come just now very vividly before me. Her childish piety certainly moves me too, but I am at times alarmed at it. When her feelings break forth, her soul sometimes appears to me like a bud that perishes before it has blown, from too strong an impulse in itself. By all that is sacred, my dear friends, don't give too much nourishment to this feeling. Probably you cannot see her so vividly in the future as I do now, with all her colours early faded, perhaps kneeling in her veil and worshipping with fruitless rosary before the image of a saint; or if not that, then dressed in the back-thrown hood and the unattractive dress, excluded from the free and glad enjoyment of life, and brooding dull and inactive in one of the Moravian Sisters' Homes. It is a dangerous time for this. Many beautiful women souls betake themselves to one or other of these silly aberrations, tearing asunder their family ties; and thus in any case, the fairest form and the richest happiness destined for woman is missed, not to mention the inner perversion of her nature, without which such things could not arise. What I fear is that the child is too much disposed to this side of things. It would be indeed an irremediable loss if that soul and spirit of hers were carried away by the corruption of a time by which it might almost be said that few women have kept themselves entirely unaffected, if that is true which Goethe says, that a stigma always clings to one who has in any way dissolved the relation of marriage or altered their religion. Such an anxiety may well be spoken out if a friend feels it, but only once; and so it may not have been without reason that I have always been prevented speaking of it till to-day, though I know not how.'

'I bear you witness,' said Ernestine, 'that you have been prevented, for I have already observed your anxious feeling more than once; and, being so definite, it might certainly have long since passed into words. But I did not encourage you in it, because I hoped you would yourself become suspicious of your idea if you saw the child more, and if her inward nature was more distinctly unfolded before you. And so then, dear friend, I appeal to your own judgment. Certainly you are quite correct in supposing that there is some inward distortion of nature involved when such a course of life is entered upon as you are anxious about. And where is this more easily to be recognised than in a child in whose case there can be so little doubt as to whether such has really arisen from within or has only been acquired from without? Can you, however, point out anything that is actually "distorted" in her, anything that goes beyond the true simplicity of childhood? Or is there some wrong relation whereby something proper to her nature has been suppressed by her pious emotions? I know nothing but that she has gone about this matter just as unreservedly as about any other that she likes and values. It is in this way that she gives herself up to every movement; and in connection with every childish interest you will find her just the same, and in this matter she has been displaying as little vanity as in any other. Besides, she has no reason for acting otherwise, and she will never have any occasion for doing so as far as we are concerned. For no one gives any special attention to it; and if she must become aware, as is natural, that we reckon this sentiment as belonging to what is highest, still no occasion is ever given for exalting such emotions or their expression in particular cases. We find her natural then; and, in fact, such sentiment is natural to her. And we think that what comes about in this way, may be also left without interference to nature.'

'And all the more certainly,' continued Elward, half

interrupting her, ' the more so that all this belongs to what is most beautiful and noble in itself. For, my dear friend, the true side of the matter must surely lie in the inward element which so possesses the little one, as she has no occasion at all to attach herself to what is merely external. This Christmas performance will be laid aside in a few days, and you know yourself very well that in our circle there is no formalism of a religious kind, no prayer at set times, no special hours of worship, but everything is done only as our heart inclines us to it. Besides, she often hears us speaking about such things, and even singing (of which she is otherwise so very fond), without joining us. All this is quite in accordance with the manner and way of children. She generally has no particular pleasure in going to church. The singing there is too poor for her taste; the rest of the service she does not understand, and it wearies her. Were there anything forced in her piety, or were she inclined to ape others, or to be led by an external authority, would she not then force herself to find what we hold so conspicuously in honour to be beautiful and worthy of sympathy? Now, as I regard all this as moving in harmony with her other development, I do not see how Romanism, or even Moravianism, could ever become attractive to her. Before such could happen, she would, in fact, have entirely to lay aside her own proper taste, which has not at all this character, as well as her almost bold and strong habit of distinguishing what is essential and chief in all things from what is its appearance and mere surrounding.'

'I would venture, however,' said Caroline, before Leonard again took up the remark, ' to deprecate the way in which you conjoin the Moravians with the Catholics.

I believe we might dispute the point as to whether the two are to be regarded as in any respect at all the same ; but at least I cannot admit the application of that fine epithet " distorted " to what pertains to the Moravians. You know I have two of my lady friends among them who are certainly not distorted, but whose judgment and understanding are as correct as their piety is deep.'

'My dear,' answered Edward, smiling, ' you must attribute this in the case of Leonard to ignorance. He merely repeats what one sometimes hears, and he has certainly never looked into a Moravian place unless to buy a good saddle, or to examine some remarkable fabric, and at the same time to get introduced to the pretty children of the Sisters' Home. I should certainly be wrong if I admitted such a thing generally. But only be good enough to observe that these remarks did not turn upon the excellences or character of the different Churches, but that we were only speaking about Sophie ; and in regard to her, any combination of these two things must appear beyond suspicion. For as you understand the matter, and without prejudice to your two lady friends, you will admit that a girl who can satisfy her religious sense in the bosom of her family and who has maintained her innocence and simplicity, will not find the world at all so dangerous ; and besides, as she has been accustomed to a joyful activity in a free life, it could not be thought that such a one without some strange aberration would shut herself up in a convent or sisters' home. Besides, as I was just about to say to Leonard, the same thing holds true of transitions both to Romanism and Moravianism, unless when they are occasioned by peculiar circumstances, such as those that you are defending. I mean that proselytes of either kind, so far as I know them, are not at all persons who have inclined to the religious life from childhood like Sophie, but, as we hear it said, it is rather pleasure-seeking women and crafty statesmen who in later years, or after certain misfortunes, become pious devotees. And so these proselytes are at least largely made up of such as have formerly dealt with whatever they have pursued, be it science, or art, or domestic life, in an entirely external way, and have wholly overlooked its relation to what is higher. Now when this relation somehow arises before their minds, they conduct themselves in this new world just like little children. They catch after its splendour, whether it be thrown from without upon the object, and magnify it, or come from an internal fire which attracts them on account of the darkness of their surroundings rather than by its own flame. And thus we may also say that in their repentance there always remains something of their sin, in that they would throw the guilt of their former coldness and darkness actually upon the Church to which they belonged, as if the sacred fire had not been preserved within it, but it had only practised a cold formalism, made up of empty words and outworn, dried-up ceremonies.'

'You may be right in fact,' replied Leonard, 'in saying that such is the case with many, but certainly this is not the only source of this evil. It appears in many cases to arise directly from within, and so it is with our little one. It is truly strange that I and others whom you are wont to call unbelievers, should have to warn you and preach to you against unbelief, but, of course, only against unbelief in superstition and all that is connected therewith. I do not need to assure you, Edward, that I

honour and love the beauty of piety, but it must be, and
continue to be, inward. If it appears outwardly so as to
form peculiar relationships in life, there springs from it
what is most hateful : a petrifying separatism and spiritual pride, the exact opposite of what piety should
properly produce. You remember, Edward, how we
lately spoke on this subject, and we considered that a
so-called spiritual profession could only be free from
danger on this side if true piety were everywhere diffused,
as is required of its professors ; and how, among the great
number whom you know from your official connections,
that you could with difficulty bring forward a couple of
examples of such who had not fallen into the latter evil.
But still more prejudicial to the laity is it when they
become zealously affected for an ostentatious piety for
which they have no special call. Indeed it appears to
me to be quite like a sort of intoxication. The piety of
the Catholics, who betake themselves to wholly external
works of piety, is only one kind of it, while that of our
own churchmen who gather themselves around some
narrow and exclusive opinion is but another. And out
of this same cup, as it appears, your little one has also
taken a draught, and it is not at all slight for such a
child. If you now foolishly favour this ambition of
becoming a holy woman, or go so far as to cherish it,
where will it in time carry her but into the convent or
to the sisterhood ? For the common run of us do not
carry out these things well in the world. And as regards
this piety that plays with the infant Christ, and the
worshipping of the aureole which she herself made for
it, is not this the most unmistakable germ of superstition ? Is it not sheer idolatry ? See to it, my dear
friends ; it is this which, if no check is put to it, will

certainly end in something irrational. But so far from putting a check upon it, I have the clearest evidence that you even give the child the Bible to read as she likes. I do, however, hope that you do not give it to her quite freely for her own use, but that you read from it in her presence, or that her mother narrates to her things from it; yet it just comes to the same thing. The mythical element must allure her fancy, and strangely confused images of a sensible kind must take a firm hold, along with which no sound conception will afterwards find a place. A sanctified letter is thus set upon the throne; and into it the unbridled arbitrariness which leads the child, will put what it never contained. Furthermore, the miraculous of itself directly nourishes superstition; and the want of connection favours every illusion of individual fanaticism and all the deceptions of a taught system. Certainly at a time when the preachers are creditably zealous in the pulpit to make the Bible as dispensable as possible, it is the worst thing that can be done to give it again into the hands of the children for whom it was never made; and it would be better for these books—to punish them as it were with one of their own sayings—that a millstone were hanged about their neck, and that they were cast into the sea where it is deepest, than that they should give offence to the little ones. What will be the result if they take the sacred history in with their other fairy tales? What dangers may not arise therefrom if the heart hangs on such a faith, and if life is to be regulated by a belief which has no other truth than this; and especially how hazardous is it for the other sex! A boy will sooner help himself out of it, and will by and by find solider ground at the right time. And if it turns out wrongly with him, then

let him only study theology for a year, and that will
certainly cure him.'

'Now,' said Edward, after he had waited to see
whether the speech was at an end, 'I must really defend
our Leonard against you who do not yet fully know
him, in order that his speech may not appear to you
more ruthless than it was meant to be. He is really
not sunk quite so deep into scepticism, and he has but
little in common with our rationalists with whom he
associates himself. But he is not yet entirely clear with
himself in this matter; and therefore he always mixes
up jest and earnest so wonderfully that it is not possible
for every one to separate them from each other. If,
however, we were to take it all in earnest, he would
certainly laugh at us not a little. I shall therefore keep
myself merely to what has been jestingly said just now,
dear friend, as what has been already stated is sufficient
for what was spoken in earnest. Let me therefore tell
you something, and don't be too much alarmed at it. It
is true that the girl does really hear much of the Bible
just as it stands. Thus Joseph has been represented to
her as only the foster-father of Christ. It is a year or
more since what I now relate occurred; and when she
put the question who then was His true father, her mother
answered that He had no other father than God. Then
she thought that God was also her father too, but that
she would not like on that account to be without me.
And that it was even a part of the suffering of Christ
that He had no right father; for it is indeed a glorious
thing to have such a one. And thereupon she caressed
me and played with my locks. You see from this how
strictly she already holds by dogmatic theology, and
what a capital capacity she has for becoming a martyr

for the faith in the immaculate conception. Nay, more than this, she actually takes the sacred history in some things as if it were mythical ; for she forms her own idea of these things when, at certain moments, the girl wins the upper hand over the child, and thus she some-times doubts of the individual facts in that history, and asks whether such a thing is indeed to be understood literally. You see this is bad enough, and that she is close upon the allegorical explanation of some of the Church Fathers.'

'Jesting in this way,' said Caroline, 'usually gives me courage to throw in a word too; and I would like to admit that she herself made the aureole around the infant Christ, and she will soon herself draw, paint, and, if possible, model the Mother and Child, but in despite and violation of all heathenly disposed artists. For already she often traces out such sketches when at her writing and reading; and thus it is done half without thinking, which is evidently so much the more Romish. But in earnest, I believe that we are only so much the safer from both extremes. For among the Moravians no importance is laid upon works of art, and therefore she would find matters too unartistic among them. And as regards the Roman Catholics, you are always saying that the best of those who have gone over from us to their Church, did it because they found there an established union of religion with the arts, which is wanting in our Church. Now Sophie has already made this union for herself in her own way ; and thus she will feel no need to attach herself to that form of it in which art often appears so strange and tasteless.'

'Ah,' said Leonard, with manifest vehemence, 'if the ladies will insist on making me appear absurd, then I

must be so through and through. And so far as I am
concerned, she may become Catholic if she likes with
her application of the arts to religion; for I don't like
that at all. I am as a Christian very unartistic, and as
an artist very unchristian. I don't like the stiff Church
which Schlegel has depicted for us somewhat stiffly in
his stanzas; nor yet do I like the poor, begging, frozen
arts being glad to find a place of refuge in it. If they
are not to be eternally young, and to live richly and
independently by themselves, forming their own world
as the ancient mythology unquestionably formed its
world, then I desire no part in them. In like manner
religion, as we regard it, appears to me to be weak and
questionable, if it wants to lean for support upon the arts.'

'Take care, Leonard,' said Ernest, 'lest your fair
friends remind you inopportunely of your own words.
Have you not lately maintained to us that life and art
are as little opposites as life and science, and that a
cultured life is properly a work of art, a beautiful
representation, the most direct union of the plastic and
the musical? Now they will say that you are not
really of opinion that life should dwell with religion or
should be inspired by it, and that religion therefore
should be nowhere but in words, where you sometimes
from all sorts of reasons need her.'

'We will not say that,' interposed Ernestine. 'Besides,
there has now been quite enough of this idle controversy,
which wearies the rest of us because we cannot share
with you in the pure delight of disputation.'

'And there we are manifestly at one,' added Edward;
'at least in the beneficent feeling which expresses itself
so specially in our life to-day. For what is this beautiful
practice of giving each other presents but a pure ex-

hibition of religious joy, which expresses itself, as joy always does, in unsought kindliness, or in giving and serving; and here, in particular, the great gift which we all equally rejoice in, is reflected in little gifts. The more purely this sentiment appears as a whole, so much the more is our own mind possessed by it. And it was on this account, dear Ernestine, that we were so delighted with your arrangement this evening, because it so appropriately gave expression to our Christmas feeling: this becoming young again, the return into the feeling of childhood, the cheerfulness of a joy in the new world which we owe to the Child who is thus celebrated. All this lay in the glimmering light of the scene, in its green flowery surroundings, and in our restrained desire.'

'Yes, indeed,' said Caroline, 'certainly what we feel in these days is so purely the religious joy in the subject itself, that I was extremely sorry at what Ernest a little ago expressed when he said it could be heightened by any glad events or expectations belonging to the outward life. But after all he was not quite in earnest in saying this. And as regards the significance of our little gifts, they have their value so far, not at all from what they refer to in particular, but only generally from their showing by such reference that the intention to give pleasure lies in them, and from their being a proof of how distinctly the image of every dear friend hovers before our mind in connection with them. My own feeling at least distinguishes that higher and more universal joy very distinctly from the liveliest interest in what may be happening or may be at hand to all of you, dear friends; and I would rather say that the latter joy is heightened by the former. If what is beautiful and gladdening stands before us at a time when we are most deeply conscious of what is the greatest and most beautiful of all things, then the latter joy will be conjoined with the former; and thus it is that all that is lovable and good obtains a greater significance when viewed in relation to the great salvation of the world. Yes, I still feel clearly, as I have formerly experienced it, that joy blossoms up within us unchecked, even along with the deepest pain; and that such joy purifies and soothes the pain without being destroyed by it, so original is it and so directly grounded upon something that is imperishable.'

'I too,' said Edward, 'who according to Ernest's former estimate would to-day perhaps have the least cause of happiness among you, do feel in myself an overflowing gladness of a purely happy and cheerful kind, which would certainly bear and endure everything that might happen. It is a mood of mind in which I could challenge fate ; or if that appears presumptuous, in which I could at least find courage for every requirement; and such a state is surely desirable for every one. I believe, however, that I owe the full consciousness and the right enjoyment of it partly to our little one, who led us a little ago to her music. For every beautiful feeling only comes completely forth when we have found the right tone for it: not the spoken word, for that at any time can only be an indirect expression—only, if I may say so, a plastic element—but the musical tone in the proper sense. In fact, music is most closely related to the religious feeling. A great deal is now said in one way or another as to how a common expression is again to be obtained for the religious feeling. But hardly any one ever thinks how that most desirable result might easily be attained, if the expression of song were again to be put into a more correct relation to that of words. What the word has made clear, the tones of music must make alive, or must convey, and fix as a harmony, into the whole inward nature.'

'No one at least will deny,' added Ernest, 'that it is only in the religious sphere that music attains its perfection. The comic species of music which exists only as a mere contrast, rather confirms than refutes this position. But an earnest opera can hardly be made at all without a religious basis; and the same would hold true of all higher works of art in musical tones, for in the subordinate artificial forms no one will seek for the spirit of the art.'

'This very close affinity,' said Edward, 'properly lies in the fact that it is only in direct relation to what is highest, or to religion, and to some particular form of it, that music, without being associated with any particular fact, obtains enough of material to be intelligible. Christianity is a unique theme exhibited in infinite variations, which, however, at the same time are connected by an internal law, and fall under definite general characters. Moreover, it is certainly true, as some one has said, that church music, although it cannot dispense with singing, might well dispense with particular words. A Miserere, a Gloria, a Requiem: what special words are needed for any one of these? It is intelligible enough by its character, and undergoes no essential change although the words are exchanged for others of similar significance, if they are only divided according to the music, and are capable of being sung; and it is all the same whether it be in the same language or in another language. In fact, no one would say that anything of importance had escaped although he had not understood the accompany-

ing words at all. Hence it is that Christianity and
music must both hold firmly to each other, because they
glorify and elevate each other. As Jesus was received
by the chorus of the angels, so do we accompany Him
with music and song on to the great hallelujah of the
Ascension; and a musical composition like Handel's
"Messiah" seems to me a compendious proclamation of
the whole of Christianity.'

'Yes, it may be said in general,' added Frederica, 'that
that is the most religious tone which penetrates most
surely into the heart.'

'And further,' added Caroline, assenting, 'that it is the
piety which sings, that ascends most gloriously and
most directly to heaven. There is nothing accidental
nor individual to sustain either of them. What Edward
has said reminds me of something which he read to us
not long since. You will at once guess to whom it
belongs. The words sounded somewhat like this, that
music never weeps or laughs over single events, but
always only over life itself.'

'We will add in Jean Paul's name,' said Edward,
'that individual occurrences are only notes of transition
for music, but its true subject is the great chords of the
heart, which, wondrously and with alternations in the
most varied melodies, always resolve themselves into the
same harmony in which are only to be distinguished the
hard and the soft, the male and the female.' ·

'See,' interposed Agnes, 'here we come again to my
former remark. What is individual and personal, be it
future or present, joy or sorrow, can give or take as little
to or from a heart which moves in moods of pious feeling,
as mere transitional notes, which leave but light traces
behind, can affect the movement of a harmony.'

'Hear me, Edward,' suddenly broke in Leonard. 'This repose of yours appears to me to be too bad. It entirely denies the reality of life, and I must call you to account for it. How can you bear it,' he continued softly, 'that Agnes can speak thus, she who lives in the most beautiful hope?'

'Why not?' she answered herself; 'is not the personal at the same time likewise here the perishable? Is not a new-born child exposed to most dangers? How easily is the mere flickering flame blown out even by the softest wind! But what is eternal in us is maternal love; it is the fundamental chord of our being.'

'And is it, then, indifferent to you,' asked Leonard, 'whether you can form your child to that which floats before you in idea, or whether it is again snatched from you in the first feeble period of life?'

'Indifferent!' she answered. 'Who says that? But the inner life, the connection of the heart, is not thus lost. And do you then believe that love is directed to what we can form the children into? What, indeed, *can* we form? No, it is directed to be beautiful and the divine which we already believe to be in them, and which every mother seeks for in every movement as soon as ever the soul of the child expresses itself.'

'Now then, my dear friends,' said Ernestine, 'in this sense every mother is again a Mary. Every mother has thus an eternal divine Child, and seeks devoutly in it for the stirrings of the higher Spirit. And into such love no fate brings any painful destruction, nor does there ever spring up within it the pernicious weed of maternal vanity. The old man may prophesy that a sword will pierce through her soul; Mary only keeps the words in her heart. The angels may rejoice, and the wise men may come and worship; yet she does not exalt herself, but always continues in the same meek and devout love.'

'Were it not,' said Leonard, 'that you express everything so charmingly, so that one cannot wish to detract from it, much might be said against your view. Otherwise, if all that held true, you would actually be the heroines of the time, you dear idealistic enthusiasts, with your contempt of what is individual and real; and we should have to lament that your circle is not stronger, and that you have not your worthy representatives in strong martial sons fit for bearing arms. You must be the true Christian Spartanesses. Look, therefore, to your words, and keep to what you promise; for there may be hard trials at hand for you so that you will have to make them good. The preparations are already complete. A great fate marches about uncertainly in our neighbourhood with strides under which the earth quakes, and we know not how it may draw us in. May then the actual with its proud arrogance only not take its revenge upon your humble contempt of it!'

'Dear friend,' answered Ernest, 'the ladies will hardly yield to us in such trials; and the whole test as it seems to me is not very much to them. What appears to us in the distance as looming huge with domestic misery, breaks down when near into many small components; what is great in it disappears, and as regards the individual, he only encounters some of these petty details, which are besides alleviated by their similarity to what is happening to all around. What must move us men in these concerns, is not what depends on nearness or distance, but just what does not fall directly within the sphere of women, and which can only arouse them through us and on our account.'

In the meantime Sophie had been mostly at the piano making closer acquaintance with her newly - acquired treasures, a part of which she did not previously know, while some of what was known she wished at once to appropriate as her own. And now she was heard singing a chorale from a cantata in a loud, clear voice,—

> He who gave us the Son that we might ever live,
> How shall He not with Him us all things freely give?

to which was attached a magnificent fugue,—

> If I possess but thee, I ask no more in heaven or earth.

When she had finished, she closed the instrument and returned into the drawing-room.

'See,' said Leonard, who saw her coming, 'here is our little prophetess! I would like to hear at once how far she already belongs to you.' Then giving her his hand, he addressed her thus: 'Tell me, little one, is it not the case that you surely like rather to be merry than sad?'

'I cannot say that I am just either of them at present,' she answered.

'What! not merry, after receiving so many pretty presents! This is certainly the effect of the solemn music. But you have not quite understood what I meant. What I asked was—and surely it was hardly necessary to ask it—which of the two you prefer to be, merry or sad?'

'Oh, that is difficult to say,' she replied; 'I am not particularly fond of being either, but I always prefer most to be what I just am at the time.'

'Now I don't understand that again, little sphinx; what do you mean by that?'

'Well,' she said, 'I know nothing further than that merriness and sadness sometimes wonderfully come together, and yet contend with each other, and that makes me anxious; because I observe, as mother has also said to me, that there is always something wrong or false in play, and therefore I don't like it.'

'Then,' he asked again, 'if you are all the one only, is it all the same to you whether you are gladsome or sad ?'

'Far from it, for I just like to be what I am ; and what I like to be is not indifferent to me. Oh, mother,' she continued, turning to Ernestine, 'do help me ; he questions me in such a strange way, and I cannot at all understand what he means. Let him rather question big people, they will be able to answer him better.'

'In fact,' said Ernestine, 'I don't think, Leonard, that you will make much further way with her. She is not at all in the habit of making comparisons about her life.'

'Don't be discouraged by this attempt,' said Ernest, encouraging him with a smile; 'catechising is always a fine art; and it is just as well practised in the courts as elsewhere. And certainly one always learns something by it, if it is not begun in an entirely erroneous way.'

'But is it possible,' said Leonard, avoiding Ernest's joking, and turning to Ernestine, 'that she has no feeling as to whether she prefers to be in a merry state or in a sad one ?'

'Who knows ?' she replied. 'What do you think, Sophie ?'

'I don't know it at all, mother; I can be very well in either; and just now I was extremely well without being the one or the other. Only he vexes me with his questions, because I cannot make out all that is to be put together in trying to answer them.'

And thereupon she kissed her mother's hand and betook herself to the opposite end of the room to her Christmas presents, where it was dimly lighted with only a few glimmering lamps.

'This at least she has clearly shown us,' said Caroline softly, 'what that childlike sense is without which one cannot enter into the Kingdom of God. It is just this, to accept every mood and every feeling for itself, and to wish to have them only pure and whole.'

'True,' said Edward, 'only she is not a mere child, and this is therefore not wholly the child sense, but she is now a girl.'

'Yes, indeed,' continued Caroline; 'and that remark should only be applicable to us. And I would only say that the lamentations which are so frequently heard from young and old, even in these very days of childish joy, that they can no longer enjoy themselves as in the years of their childhood, certainly do not arise from those who have had such a childhood. Only yesterday I could not but wonder at the astonishment of some to whom I asserted that I was still as capable of lively joy as ever, only in more abundance.'

'Yes,' said Leonard jestingly; 'and the poor child is often regarded as vain by people of that kind, even when she does nothing but rejoice in a truly childlike way about something that is girlish. But never mind, my fair friend, these gainsayers are in turn just those to whom nature has assigned a second childhood at the end of life, in order that, when they reach this goal, they may have a last consoling draught from the beaker of joy at the close of their long, pitiable, and joyless time.'

'This is truly more solemn and tragic than ludicrous,' said Ernest. 'I at least hardly know anything more dreadful than the way in which the great mass of men proceed in view of the fact that they must necessarily lose the first objects of the delight of their childhood. Owing to their incapability of attaining to higher things, they become thoughtlessly indifferent to the beautiful development of life, and are tormented with ennui. I hardly know whether to say they merely look on at life or participate in it, for even that is too much for their utter inactivity. And so their life goes on, till at last out of its nothingness there arises a second childhood, which, however, is related to the first as a cross - tempered dwarf is to a beautiful and lovable child, or as the unsteady flicker of a dying flame is to the lustre of one that has just been kindled and is spreading all round and transforming itself into many forms.'

'Only against one thing,' said Agnes, 'would I like again to raise an objection. Is it then the case that the first childish objects of enjoyment must, in fact, be lost that the higher may be gained? May there not be a way of obtaining the latter without letting the former go? Does life then begin with a pure illusion in which there is no truth at all, and nothing enduring? How am I rightly to comprehend this? In the case of the man who has come to reflect upon himself and the world, and who has found God, seeing that this process is not gone through without conflict and warfare, do his joys rest upon the eradication, not merely of what is evil, but of what is blameless? For it is thus we always indicate the childlike, or even the childish, if you will rather so have it. Or is it the case that time with some peculiar poison must already have slain the first original joys of life? And the transition from the one state into the

C

other, must it proceed then in every case through what has really nothing in it?'

'You may well call it nothing,' remarked Ernestine; 'and yet it appears that men—and they also confess it themselves, and one might almost say the best of them confess it most—as such generally lead between childhood and their better existence a life that is strange, wild, passionate, and confused. On the one side, it looks like a continuation of their childhood, the joys of which also show a violent and destructive nature; but on the other side it shapes itself into an unsteady striving, an unsettled and always changing, a letting go and trying to lay hold of things in life, of which we women understand nothing. In our sex the two tendencies are combined with each other in a less perceptible way. In what attracts us in the sports of childhood our life already lies implied, only that as we grow up there is gradually revealed the higher meaning of this and that. And even when we understand God and the world in our own way, we express our highest and sweetest feelings always again in those lovable trifles, in that mild brightness, which made us friendly with the world in the days of childhood.'

'Hence,' said Edward, 'men and women also have in the development of the spiritual nature, although it must be the same in both, their different ways in order that they may also be united in this relation through complementary knowledge. Indeed it may well be the case, and it seems to me clearly to be so, that the opposition of the unconscious and the reflective appears more strongly in us men, and it reveals itself during the process of transition in that restless striving and that passionate struggle with the world and ourselves; whereas in your calm and gracious nature the balance of the two elements and their inner unity comes to light: and holy earnestness and amiable playfulness are with you everywhere identical.'

'But then,' rejoined Leonard, smiling slyly, 'strangely enough, we men should be more Christian than you women. For Christianity speaks everywhere of a process of conversion, of a change of mind, of becoming new, whereby what is old has to be expelled. Of all which, if the foregoing speech is true, women, a few Magdalenes excepted, would have no need at all.'

'But Christ Himself,' rejoined Caroline, 'has not been converted. And on this very account He has always been the protector and patron of women; and whereas you men have only contended about Him, we have loved and reverenced Him. Now what could you object to this, if I were to say that we have only put the right sense into the antiquated proverb that we always continue to be children, whereas you men must first be converted in order that you may become so again?'

'And to apply the suggestion to what is on hand,' added Ernest, 'what is the celebration of the infancy of Jesus but the distinct recognition of the immediate union of the Divine with what belongs to the child, in consequence of which union the child needs no further conversion? Agnes has likewise already expressed it as the common view of all women, that in their children, even from their birth, they assume the presence of the Divine, and seek for it as the Church seeks it in Christ.'

'Yes, this very festival,' said Frederica, 'is the nearest and best proof that it really stands with us as Ernestine has already indicated.'

'How so?' asked Leonard.

'Because,' she replied, 'small portions of the nature of our joy which are yet neither unnoticeable nor forgotten, may be examined in order to see whether it has experienced any such sudden transformations. It can hardly be necessary to put the question to our conscience, for the thing speaks for itself. It is evident enough that everywhere women and girls are the souls of these little festivals; they are the most busied about them, and are also the most purely receptive of their influence, and have the highest delight in them. If such things were left to you men only, they would soon perish; it is through us alone that they become a perpetual tradition. 'But, it may be asked, could we not have the religious joy alone by itself; and should that not be so, it may further be asked whether we had found it out at a later stage as something new? But in our case everything about this festival goes on now just as in earlier years. In childhood we already assigned a peculiar significance to these presents; to us they were more than the same things given at another time. It was only so because even then there was a dim mysterious presentiment of what has since gradually become clearer, and which always still arises most lovingly before us in the same form, and will not let the accustomed symbol go. Indeed, in view of the exactness with which the little beautiful moments of life remain in our memory, it would be possible to trace out from stage to stage the unfolding of the higher relation.'

'Truly,' said Leonard, 'were it vividly and well done, as you well can do it, it would certainly give us a lovely series of little pictures if you were to describe to us your several Christmas joys, with their memorable incidents; and those even who may not enter with special sympathy into the immediate object, would still be pleased with your effort.'

'How prettily he gives us to understand that it would be wearisome to himself!' cried Caroline.

'Assuredly,' said Ernestine, 'this might be too trivial, even for one who wished to be ever so gallant, as well as for those who really had more mind for the subject. But whoever can relate any single incident, remarkable in any way, bearing a reference to our conversation, pray let it be done; and let it be joined on by the teller to an incident of the kind belonging to my early childhood, which I will now tell you, although perhaps some of you may already know it.'

Frederica arose and said, 'You know that I am not in the habit of relating things in this way. I shall, however, do something else which may give you pleasure. I will take my place at the piano, and follow your narratives with my fantasias upon them. Thus you will also hear something from me, and with your finer and higher ear.'

Ernestine began : 'It so happened that just before the joyous festival, on the occasion I refer to, all sorts of sad circumstances and complications had occurred which had but shortly before turned out happily in the end. Hence it was that there was far less provision made than usual for the enjoyment of the children, nor could there be so much love and care bestowed upon such preparations as were usually made. This was a favourable opportunity for getting a wish satisfied which I had expressed the previous year, but in vain. At that time the so-called Christmas carols were held in the late hours of the evening in the churches, and they were continued even till near midnight, the singing alternating with addresses to an audience that was always changing, and not very deeply engaged in devotion. After some hesitation, I was allowed to go to church accompanied by my mother's maid - servant in charge of me. I hardly remember of ever experiencing such mild weather at Christmas as was at that time. The sky was clear, and yet the evening felt almost warm. In the neighbourhood where the Christmas market was held, and which was already almost over, there roamed about large bands of boys provided with the last of the pipes, whistling-birds, and spinning-tops, which had been cleared off at a cheap price, and they were running about making much noise on the ways that led to the different churches. It was not till we came quite close that we heard the organ and the voices of a few children and old people accompanying it in an irregular way. Notwithstanding a considerable display of lamps and tapers, the dim pillars and walls grown grey with age could not be clearly seen, and I could only with difficulty make out a few shapes, which, however, presented nothing that was gladdening to the eye. Still less could the clergyman with his quavering voice inspire me with any interest. Quite dissatisfied, I was about to ask my companion to return, and was just casting a last look everywhere round about me. Then in an open pew under a beautiful old monument I noticed a lady with a little child upon her bosom. She appeared to give little heed to the preacher, or the music, or to anything else around her, but seemed to be deeply sunk in her own thoughts alone, and her eyes were directed fixedly upon the child, who drew me irresistibly towards her, and my companion led me up. Here I had all at once found the sanctuary that I had been long seeking in vain. I stood before the noblest figure that I had ever seen. The lady was simply dressed, and it seemed as if her tall and graceful and distinguished form turned the open pew into a closed chapel. There was no one near, and yet she did not appear to observe me, even when I stood close before her. Her mien seemed to me at one time to be cheerful and at another to be sad, her breathing now trembling with joy and again hardly suppressing joyful sighs; but the enduring impression of the whole was friendly repose and loving devotion; and this feeling streamed gloriously from her large black downcast eye, which the lashes would have entirely hidden from me had I been any taller. The child also appeared to me uncommonly lovable; it looked animated and yet quiet in its movements, and it seemed to me as if engaged in a half unconscious dialogue of love and longing with its mother. And now I had living forms corresponding to the beautiful pictures of Mary and the Child, and I became so absorbed in this fancy that half involuntarily I drew the dress of the lady to me and asked with a moved and pleading voice, May I then give a gift to the dear child? Thereupon I poured out upon his clothes some handfuls of dainties which I had taken with me as a resource against whatever need might come. The lady looked closely at me for a moment, then drew me in a kindly way to herself, kissed my brow, and said, " Oh yes, my little darling; everybody is giving away to-day, and all on account of a Child." I kissed the hand she laid upon my neck, and the little outstretched hand of the child, and was about to go quickly away, when she said, " Wait; I will also present you with something; it may be that I shall again recognise you by it." She searched about and drew from her hair a gold pin with a green stone, which she fastened to my cloak. I again kissed her dress, and quickly left the church with a full heart and a feeling of bliss beyond anything. She turned out to be Edward's eldest sister, that glorious tragic form, and she has had a greater influence than any other upon my life and upon my inward nature. She soon became the friend and guide of my youth; and although I have had nothing to share with her but sorrows, I yet regard my connection with her as belonging to the most beautiful and important elements of my life. Edward also stood on that occasion as a grown - up boy behind her, but without being at all observed by me.'

Frederica appeared to have known the subject of her narration, so exactly did her playing accompany the graceful story, and thus she brought every part of it at the same time into harmony with the impression of the whole. When Ernestine had finished, Frederica, after some fantastic variations, glided into a beautiful church melody. Sophie, who at once made it out, ran up to join her voice, and they sang together the beautiful verses of Novalis,—

> I see thee in a thousand forms,
> O Mary, lovingly express'd;
> Yet none can show thy deeper charms
> That move the soul within my breast.
>
> I only know the world's uproar
> Appears now as a vanished dream;
> And joys of Heaven, unknown before,
> Through all my heart for ever stream.

'Mother,' said Sophie, when she went back, 'all that now stands vividly before me which you have sometimes told me about aunt Cornelia and the beautiful youth whom I once saw, who died so heroically, but in vain, for the cause of freedom. But let me bring the pictures; we all know them well, yet I think we must now look at them again.'

The mother nodded assent, and the child fetched two pictures, painted by Ernestine, but not yet framed. They both represented her friend and the son of her sorrow. The one represented him returning to her from the battle wounded, but covered with glory, the other as he taking farewell of her when about to fall as one of the last sacrifices of that most bloodthirsty time.

Leonard interrupted the painful memories which found expression in only a few sad words by turning to Agnes and saying, 'Tell us something else, child ; and free us thereby from the sense of keen pain which does not properly belong to our joy, and from the Mariolatry into which these two have now sung us.'

'Well, then,' replied Agnes, 'I will relate something that is less important, but perhaps it will have its compensation in its gladsomeness. You know a year ago we were all scattered at the time of this festival, and for some weeks I had been staying with my brother to help Louisa, who had had her first child. The holy evening had also begun there, according to our habit, with an assembly of friends. Louisa was entirely recovered, but I had to undertake to arrange everything ; and to my joy there prevailed among all the pure cheerfulness and the freshly stirred love which everywhere springs up on this general day of joy among good men. And as this cheerfulness clothes itself with gifts and tokens of gladness in the very vesture of mirth and free playsome childlikeness, so was it likewise among us. Suddenly the nurse appeared in the drawing-room with her child, went peering round the tables, and called out several times half-jesting, half-whimpering, "Has, then, no one made a present to the child ; have they, then, all forgotten the baby ?" We immediately gathered round about the little

gracious creature ; and all sorts of expressions broke out
in jest and earnest as to how, with all our love, we could
yet give to him no joy, and how right it had been that
we had bestowed everything which specially related to
him upon the mother. And now the nurse was shown
all his presents, and they were also held up to the little
one : the little caps and stockings, the clothes, spoons,
and napkins, and such like. But neither the splendour
and sound of the noble metal, nor the dazzling, trans-
parent white of the material, appeared to move his senses.
So indeed it is, children, I said to the others ; he is still
entirely his mother's, and even she can to-day stir in
him but the usual daily feeling of satisfaction. His
consciousness is still united with hers ; in her it dwells,
and only in her can we cherish and gladden it. " But,"
said an amiable girl, " we have been all very limited
in our views, in that we have thought in this way
only for the present moment. Does not, then, the whole
life of the child stand before its mother ? " With these
words she begged me to give up the keys ; several others
scattered away in like manner with the assurance that
they would soon be back again ; and Ferdinand told
them to make haste, for he also had something else in
view for the little one. " You will not easily guess what
it is ? " said he to us who remained. " I am going at once
to baptize him ; I could think of no moment more beautiful
for it than this ; provide what is necessary, and I shall
also be back when our friends return." As quickly as
possible we dressed the child with what was most
graceful among the presents, and we had hardly finished
when those who had gone away returned with all sorts
of gifts. They presented a wonderful mixture of jest
and earnestness, such as cannot but be in any attempts

to represent the future. There was material for making articles of clothing, not only for his boyhood, but even for his marriage day ; a toothpick and a watch-chain, with the wish that it might be said of him in a better sense than was done of Churchill, when he plays with his watch-chain or uses his toothpick there comes forth a poem ; there was also fashionable note-paper on which he might write the first letter to his sweetheart; elementary text-books for all sorts of languages and sciences; and also a Bible, which was to be handed to him when the first instruction in Christianity was given to him ; and his uncle, who is fond of caricatures, even brought as the first requisite of a future dandy, as he expressed it, a pair of spectacles, and did not rest till they were put on before the large bright blue eyes of the little one. This caused great laughter and jesting ; but Louisa asserted quite earnestly, with the exception of the spectacles— for he must certainly have her and Ferdinand's excellent eyes—that she saw him now quite vividly and with definite form and features, in a certain genuine prophetic way, before her in all the times and relations to which the presents pointed. It was in vain that they joked with her as to how old-fashioned he would probably turn out if he should really honour every present by using it, and how in particular the writing-paper must be taken care of lest it became yellow. At last we agreed that the giver of the Bible was to be praised above all, for this he would most certainly be able to use. I drew their attention to the dress we had put on the little one, yet no one found anything peculiar in this, but only that he had received their gifts in a right worthy manner. Hence they were all not a little astonished when Ferdinand entered the room in his full canonicals, while the table with the water was brought at the same time. " Don't be too much astonished, dear friends," he said. " The remark of Agnes some time ago very naturally suggested the thought of baptizing the boy on this day. You will all be witnesses, and thereby you will anew subscribe yourselves as sympathizing friends of his life." " You have presented him with gifts," he continued, after he had looked at them individually amid many cheerful remarks ; " they refer to a life of which he yet knows nothing, just as gifts were presented to Christ which pointed to a glory of which the Child yet knew nothing. Let us now make what is most beautiful his own, even Christ Himself, although it can bring to him as yet no joy or enjoyment. Not in the mother alone nor in me alone will there now dwell for him henceforth the power of the higher life, which cannot yet be in himself, but it will be in us all ; and out of us all it must betimes stream to him, and he must receive it into himself." He thus gathered us around him, and almost straightway from the conversation he went on to the sacred act. With a slight allusion to the words, " Can any forbid that these be baptized ? " he proceeded to say how that the very fact that a Christian child is received by love and joy, and always continues surrounded by them, furnishes a guarantee that the Spirit of God will dwell in him ; how the birthday festival of the new world must be a day of love and joy ; and how the union of both is specially adapted to consecrate a child of love to the higher birth of the divine life. When we had then laid all our hands upon the child, according to the good old practice in those parts, it was as if the rays of heavenly love and joy had concentrated upon the head and heart of the child as in a new focus ; and it was certainly our common feeling that they kindled there a new life, and that they would thus ray out again on all sides.'

'Again just as before,' interrupted Leonard; 'only we have this time as it were an inverted negative Christian child which the aureole streams into, not out from.'

'You have touched it off splendidly,' answered Agnes; 'I could not have said it so finely. It is the mother whose love sees the whole man in the child; and this love which calls to her as with an English greeting, is even such that it sees the heavenly radiance already streaming out from her child, and only upon her prophetic face is that beautiful reflection formed which Sophie has represented in an unconscious childish way. And you will also say better and finer than I can, if you only say it at all, why it is that I have given up this evening again to you; for I am not able to describe in words how deeply and fervently I have felt that every cheerful joy is religion; that love, leisure, and devotion are tones of a perfect harmony which in every way can follow and accord with each other. And, Leonard, if you will do what is very clever, take care not to jest; for then the truth will certainly come to you against your will as before.'

'And why should I?' answered Leonard. 'You have yourself stated how you would have it expressed, namely, not by words, but in music. But as it appears Frederica has herself done nothing but listen, and has given us nothing at all to hear, not even your symbol, with which you were just now so enchanted—the simple accord; how is this accounted for?'

'Truly,' said Frederica, 'it is easier to accompany at once a narrative like the former one; especially if one

happens to know something of it,' she added, smiling.
'But I believe furthermore that my art will be less lost
on you if I only follow the narration; and if you will,
it shall now be played directly over to you.' She
played a fantasy on the theme, inweaving the music of
some cheerful, bright church melodies, which, however,
are now little heard; and then sang, in order to finish
again with her favourite poet, Novalis, some of the
verses of his hymn,—

> Where stayst Thou, world's Consoler, still?
> Long waits the room which Thou must fill,—

naturally selecting those stanzas which appealed most
to the female heart:

> O Father, send Him forth with power;
> Give from Thy hand this richest dower;
> But pureness, love, and shame divine
> Have long kept back this Child of Thine. . . .

> The winter wanes; a new year nigh
> Stands by His crib, an Altar High;
> It is the whole world's first New Year,
> That with this Child doth now appear.

> Dim eyes behold the Saviour true,
> The Saviour lights those eyes anew;
> His head the fairest flowers adorn,
> From which He shines like smiling morn.

> He is the Star; He is the Sun;
> The Fount whence streams eternal run;
> From herb and stone and sea and light,
> Shines forth His radiant vision bright.

> Through all things gleams His infant play;
> Such warm young love will ne'er decay;
> He twines Himself, unconscious, blest,
> With endless power to every breast. . . .

Where a break came in, she was able to fill it up with harmonies that expressed the inward rest and the pleasure with which she was filled, and which she wished to represent.

'Now, however,' said Caroline, 'you will have to prepare to pass to tones of sadness, although you may have to end with pure joy. You will now have from me too a sketch set in the same frame around this beautiful festival. For I feel disposed to relate to you how I celebrated the festival last year at the home of my dear friend Charlotte. There is properly nothing at all in the way of narrative to give in connection with it. It is only a contribution to what you already know of Charlotte from other narrations and from her letters; and you must recall everything which you already know about her. In her part of the country, the amusing habit prevails among the grown - up people of making their presents to each other without letting themselves be known. By the most roundabout ways, and in the strangest manner, each one makes his gift come to the other, whenever it is possible, disguising it under some-thing less important, so that the receiver of the gift has sometimes been made to rejoice or to wonder, and yet has not found out the right person. There must thus be a great deal of planning and devising; and the happy scheme is often not carried out without varied and long preparations. Charlotte, however, had for several weeks to bear the sorrow of an inexplicable, and therefore so much the more distressing, sickness of her darling boy, her youngest child. For a long time the physician could neither give nor take hope, while pain and want of rest always robbed the little angel more and more of his strength ; and so there was nothing but his dissolution expected. Among the friends, both male and female, all the preparations that had been entered upon to give the mother a surprise by ingenious conceits or playful jest, were interrupted with inward sorrow. No one would venture even by a single gift to try to turn away her attention from the object of her love and pain; everything was deferred to a more favourable time. She almost incessantly carried the child about in her arms; she never lay down at night for her usual rest; only in the daytime, when the child appeared calmer, and when she could entrust it to me or to another intimate friend, did she allow herself short snatches of repose. Nevertheless she did not neglect looking after the matters connected with the festival, however often we entreated her not to exhaust herself any more with what was so much in contrast to her anxieties. It was certainly impossible for her to do any work herself, but she planned and arranged; and she often surprised me in the midst of her deepest pain by putting a question as to whether this or that was provided, or by again expressing the thought of some new little pleasure. There was certainly no mirthfulness or playfulness in anything she said, but neither is that generally in accordance with her nature. There was no want, however, of thoughtfulness, or of attention to what was important; and in all there was the quiet grace which characterizes all her actions. I still remember when I once, almost disapprovingly, expressed my wonder, that she said to me: "My good friend, there is no fairer nor more befitting frame round a deep sorrow than a chain of little joys prepared by us for others. Everything is then in the setting in which it can remain for life; and why should we not wish to get at once into this setting? There is something imperfect in all that time effaces; and it does this in the case of all that is violent and one-sided." A few days before Christmas, it could be seen that there was an internal struggle going on within her. She was almost the only one who had not yet been convinced of the hopeless state of the child; but now his looks, and particularly his weakness, overpowered her. The image of death arose all at once and most definitely before her. Deeply absorbed in herself, she paced about for an hour, carrying the child in her arms, and showing all the signs of deepest emotion. She gazed for a while with a sadly illuminated countenance upon it, as for the last time; bent down for a long kiss upon his brow; and then with new strength and courage she reached me her hand, and said: "Now I have overcome it, dear friend. I have given back the little angel to the Heaven from whence he came, I now look calmly for his dissolution. I am calm and assured; nay, I can even wish to see him soon depart, in order that the signs of pain and of destruction may not dim the angelic form which has impressed itself so deeply and for ever upon my soul." On the morning of the day before Christmas, she gathered the children around her, and asked them whether they would celebrate their festival on that day, saying that everything was ready, and that it all depended on themselves; or whether they would wait till little Edward was buried, and the first stillness and the first pain should be past. They declared unanimously that they could find no pleasure in anything, but that the little brother was still living, and even might not die. In the afternoon, Charlotte handed me the child, and lay down to rest. She fell into a long,

D

refreshing sleep, from which I had resolved not to awaken her, whatever might happen. Then there came a crisis in the almost dying body, accompanied by violent convulsions, which I regarded as the last, and it indicated to the physician, when he had been called, both the evil and the cure. After an hour, the child was found to be evidently better, and it was distinctly seen that it was on the way of recovery. The children hastily decorated the room and the couch of the little one in a festal manner. The mother then entered, and she believed that we were only trying to beautify the appearance of the dead body. When she looked upon the couch, the first smile of the child gleamed upon her. Like a half-dead bud rising again after a kindly shower, and unfolding itself to the sun, so did the child appear to her among the flowers. "If it is no delusive hope," said she, embracing us all after she had learned what had occurred, "then this is a different regeneration from what I had expected. I had hoped and prayed," she continued, "that the child might be raised out of this earthly life during these festival days. It moved me sadly and soothingly to send an angel to Heaven at the time when we celebrate the sending of the greatest One to the earth. And now both of them come to me at the same time, sent directly from God. At this festival of the regeneration of the world, the darling of my heart is born again to a new life. Yes, he lives; there is no doubt of it," she said, as she bent over him, yet hardly dared to touch him, or to press her lip to his hand. "May he continue to be such an angel," she said, after a pause, "purified by suffering as if he had passed through death, and been consecrated to a higher life. He is to me a gift of special grace, a heavenly child, because I had already consecrated him to Heaven."'

Caroline had to tell many things connected with this history more precisely, as well as to give a further account of the rare excellence of her friend to whom she was devoted with such special regard. Leonard listened with quite a peculiar interest, and was almost vexed when Ernest asked him : ' But do you not find here again the same thing as before, as it were an inverted Mary who begins with the deepest maternal suffering, with the *Stabat Mater*, and ends with joy in the divine Child ? '

' Or indeed, not inverted at all,' said Ernestine ; ' for Mary's pain could not but vanish in the feeling of the divine greatness and glory of her Son ; just as, on the other hand, from the commencement of her faith and her hopes, everything that outwardly occurred to her could only appear as suffering, as alienation.'

At this point the conversation was interrupted by the entrance of a merry party of acquaintances, some of whom did not belong to any particular company, while others had exhausted their own sources of enjoyment more rapidly from their unsettled feeling ; and now they were roaming about to take a glance here and there as to how their friends had been enjoying themselves, and what gifts had been given and received. In order to be more welcome as spectators, and that they might find everywhere a friendly reception, they announced themselves as messengers of Father Christmas, and distributed the choicest dainties for the palate among the boys and girls. Sophie was spared the usual ceremonial of the inquiry about the good behaviour of the children, and she attached herself readily and pleasantly to the new arrivals.

She quickly renewed the illumination of her tableaux, and was as eloquent a guide as she was a curious questioner about all that her friends had already seen elsewhere. A hurried refreshment was handed round, and then the visitors hastened away, expressing a wish to be joined by some of the members of the company. This, however, Edward would not allow. He said they must all remain for some time yet together; and, besides, Joseph was certainly expected, and he had received the promise that he should find them all there.

When the visitors had departed, Ernest said, ' Well, as it has now been resolved that we shall spend the evening here in conversation and at table, I think we owe the ladies something in return, that they may be the more willing to stay with us. However, the art of narrating is not the gift of men; and for my part, I should be the last to persuade myself to presume upon it. But what think you, friends, of this ? Suppose that after an English, not to say a Greek fashion, and one which is not quite strange to us, we were to choose a subject about which it would be incumbent on every one to say something ? And further, that it should be a subject of such a kind that in discussing it we would not have to forget the presence of the ladies, but rather regard it as our best aim to be understood and praised by them ? '

All agreed to this proposal; and the ladies were delighted with it, because they had not heard such a thing for long.

' Well then,' said Leonard, ' if you ladies enter with such interest into the proposal, you must also give the subject upon which we are to discourse, lest in our awkwardness we should be taking up something that might be too far away, or uninteresting to you.'

'If the others are of the same opinion,' said Frederica, 'and if it were not to cause you too much inconvenience, I should like to propose as your subject the Christmas Festival itself, as it is that which keeps us gathered together here. It has so many sides of interest, that each one may glorify it in such a way as may be most agreeable to himself.'

No one made any objection to this, and Ernestine observed that any other subject would have appeared strange, and have in a manner destroyed the evening.

'Well then,' said Leonard, 'in accordance with our custom, I, as the youngest present, cannot refuse to be the first speaker. And I will be the first the more willingly, partly because the impression of an imperfect discourse will be the more easily taken away by a better, and partly because I shall most certainly enjoy the pleasure of anticipating some of the first thoughts of the others. At the same time,' he added, smiling, 'your arrangement doubles the number of the discoursers on the subject to you this year, in an invisible way ; for you will hardly fail to attend church to-morrow, and it would rather be a vexation to us than a pleasure to the worthy men who will discourse to you there, and perhaps a very great weariness to yourselves, if you had to hear the same thing over again in the churches. Hence I will keep myself as far away as possible from their lines; and so I begin my discourse.

'Everything may be glorified and extolled in either of two ways: first, it may be commended, by which I mean that its nature and essential character may be recognised and represented as good ; but, secondly, it may be eulogised, that is to say, its excellence and perfection in its own kind may be put prominently forward. Now the first method may be here passed over, and it may be left to others to praise the festival as such generally, and so far as it is a good thing, that by certain actions and usages returning at appointed times the remembrance of great events shall be secured and preserved. But if there are to be any such festivals at all, and if the primary origin of Christianity is to be regarded as something great and important, then no one can deny that this festival of Christmas is an admirable festival, so perfectly does it realize its purpose, and under such difficult conditions. For if it were to be said that the remembrance of the birth of the Redeemer is far better preserved by the mere Scriptures themselves and by instruction in Christianity generally than by the Festival, then I would venture to deny this. For us, indeed, who may claim to belong to the more educated class, it seems to me that the former medium might perhaps be enough, but this would by no means be the case with the great mass of the uneducated people. For not to mention the Roman Church, where the Scriptures are little or not at all put into their hands, but confining our consideration to those of our own communion, it is manifest how little they are disposed to read the Bible, or are even capable of understanding it in its proper connection. What of it is imprinted upon their memory in the course of the instruction they receive, is rather made up of the proofs of separate propositions than the history as such; while, on the other hand, what is got by them from the history in this way is rather the death of the Redeemer, which is thus brought into remembrance, and those parts of His life which are imitable and instructive in detail, rather than His first entrance into the world.

Nay more, even in reference to the life of the Redeemer, I would venture to assert that the facility with which we believe in the miracles performed by Him has its foundation chiefly in our festival and the impressions which it produces. For it is manifest that the belief in the miraculous much rather arises in this way than through the medium of evidences or doctrine. Otherwise, how comes it that the Roman Catholic Christian believes so much in the miracles of his saints although verging on the absurd, yet could not resolve to believe in anything similar, however similar it may be represented to him to be, if it is connected with persons belonging to an alien religion or a different historical circle, although at the same time the miracles of his own saints are not at all really connected with the proper truths and obligations of the Christian faith? In fact, he believes all this just because of the festivals which have been instituted in honour of these saints; for what in the form of mere narrative would by itself exercise no convincing power is brought by these festivals into connection with the impressiveness of a sensible present fact, and thereby obtains a hold and always establishes itself anew in his heart. Thus it is that in ancient times much of the marvellous and miraculous relating to the dim early ages, was mainly preserved in this way, and came to be believed through the festivals; and this holds even of such things as the historians and poets say little or nothing of. Indeed, action is so much more effective than words for this purpose, that not seldom it was on account of festal actions and usages, when their true meaning had been lost, that false histories were not only invented but came to be also believed. And, conversely, we have analogous instances in the Christian Church where fables have been devised in order to heap up the miraculous to an increased degree, and they have only really come to be believed when festivals came to be consecrated to them. The Ascension of Mary may be taken as an example. If, then, the common people hold so much more to actions and customs than to narrative and doctrine, we have every reason to believe that even among ourselves the belief in the miraculous connected with the appearance of the Redeemer finds its point of attachment chiefly in our festival and its favourite usages. And as regards the Roman Church, in addition to this all that relates to Mary comes in aid, because she is always hailed and addressed as the Virgin. This then, and all that depends upon it, is the merit for which I first of all extol and eulogize our Festival.—But I have further indicated that this memorial relates to a subject which has been specially difficult to preserve, and that the merit of it is therefore so much the greater. I will make clear what I mean. The more any one generally knows about an object, the more definitely and significantly does he represent it to himself; and the more necessary its connection with the present is, so much the easier does every institution become whose aim is to recall it. The case, however,—as it appears to me,—is very much otherwise in reference to all that pertains to the first appearance of Christ. I allow Christianity to be regarded as unquestionably a strong and powerful present fact, but [the earthly personal activity of Christ appears to me to be far less connected with it than most people rather assume than believe.] In particular, what rests upon Him in reference to the reconciliation of our race, is connected by all of us specially with His death; and in this connection—as I think—more turns upon an eternal decree of God than upon a particular individual fact; and on this account we ought to connect these ideas not so much with one particular moment of time, but rather to extend them beyond the temporal history of the Redeemer, and hold them as symbolical. Yet it is natural that the idea of a memorial in remembrance of the death of Christ, which was the sign of the completed redemption, as well as a memorial of His resurrection as the authentication of that completed redemption, could not but for ever establish themselves among His believing followers. The resurrection was on that account also the chief subject of the first evangelization, and the foundation upon which the Church was built, so that it perhaps might not have been necessary continually to recall its remembrance even by the weekly celebration of Sunday. But if, apart from the idea of the atonement, we consider the human activity of Christ, the substance of which is only to be sought in the proclamation of His doctrine and in the founding of the Christian fellowship, it is wonderful how little is the share which can rightly be ascribed to Him in the present form of our Christianity. Only consider how little of its doctrine as well as of its institutions can be directly referred to Himself, whereas by far the most of them is of other and later origin. So much is this the case, that if we think of John the Forerunner, Christ Himself, the Apostles, including the late-comer, and then the early fathers, as forming the members of a series, it must be admitted that the second member of the series does not stand in the middle between the first and third, but that Christ is far closer to John the Baptist than to Paul. Indeed it remains doubtful whether it was at all in accordance with Christ's will that such an exclusive and organized Church should be everywhere formed, although without it our present Christianity—and consequently also our festival, the subject of my discourse—cannot be conceived of. On this account the earthly life of Christ was also put greatly in the background in the first proclamation of Christianity; and as most people now believe, it was only proclaimed in part by subordinate persons. Furthermore, if we note the zealous striving of these narratives to attach Christ to the old royal House of the Jewish people, which, whether the relation be so or not, is nevertheless quite unimportant as regards the founder of a universal religion, it must be admitted that His life was narrated only in a subordinate manner. Christ's supernatural birth, however, appears still less to have been universally spread by historical narratives,] otherwise there could not have been at the time so many Christians who regarded Him as a naturally produced man. And hence the truth only appears to have been brought forth out of the rubbish, and to have again become predominant, by means of our festival. For in the conflict of the different opinions the narrative by itself would not have sufficed, as the narrators, if they gave no consideration to this diversity of opinion, could decide nothing; but if otherwise, then to a certain extent they would be themselves transformed from witnesses and narrators into parties. For this diversity is so great, that however we may designate it, every narrative or assertion undoes the other. Or can any assert the resurrection, without being compelled to leave it free for every one to explain the death as not having happened?—which, indeed, can mean nothing else than that the later fact explains the opinion to be false which had been held regarding the earlier facts. In like manner,

again, the Ascension of Christ makes the truth of
His life to be in a manner suspected. For the life
belongs to the planet, and what can be separated from
it cannot have borne a living connection with it. As
little result remains if the opinion of those who denied
Christ a true body or a true human soul, is taken along
with the opinion of those who, on the contrary, would
not attribute to Him true deity, or generally what is
superhuman. Nay more, if we reflect that it is disputed
as to whether He is still present on earth only in a spiritual and divine way, or likewise also in a corporeal and
sensible manner, both parties may be easily brought to
this, that their common and hidden meaning is that
Christ was not present nor lived upon earth and among
His followers of yore in another or more peculiar
manner than He does now. In short, what is presented
in experience and history regarding the personal existence of Christ, has become so uncertain by the diversity
of opinions and doctrines maintained on the subject, that
if our festival must be pre-eminently regarded as the
foundation of the belief which has been maintained in
common regarding Him, it is thereby glorified all the
more, and there is demonstrated a power in it bordering
closely upon that fact already mentioned, namely, that
history itself is sometimes really made by such usages.
But what in all this is most to be wondered at, and what
may at once serve us as an example and a reproach in
reference to many other things, is this, that the festival
evidently owes its prevalence for the most part to the
circumstance that it has been introduced into our houses
and homes, and that it has been established among the
children. It is there, in fact, where we ought to establish
what is most valuable and sacred to us ; and we should

regard it as discreditable and a bad sign that we do not
do so.—This institution, then, we will maintain as it has
been handed down to us; and the less we know as to
what its wonderful power lies in, the less shall we change
even the least element in it. To me at least, even its
smallest details are full of significance. For as a Child
is its chief subject, so it is also the children above all
who exalt and maintain the festival, and through the
festival also Christianity itself. And as night is the
historical cradle of Christianity, so the festival of its
birth is also celebrated in the night; and the lighted
tapers with which it sparkles are, as it were, the star
above the inn, as well as the aureole without which the
Child would not be found in the darkness of the manger,
or in the otherwise starless night of history. And as it
is dark and doubtful as to what we have acquired in the
person of Christ, and from whom we have got it; so
also the practice, which I have learned about from the
second last narrative, is the most beautiful and the most
symbolical form of the giving of Christmas presents.
This is my honest opinion, to which I now challenge you
to respond by emptying a beaker to the perpetual con-
tinuance of our festival; and I am the more certain of
your joining me with approval in this from hoping you
may thus make up for all else, and wash away what may
have appeared to you blameable in my discourse.'

' I now understand,' said Frederica, ' why he made so
little objection to our theme, the unbelieving knave that
he is, as he had a mind to speak so wholly against
our proper meaning regarding it. I would like to
press for his receiving condign punishment, all the more
because I proposed the subject, and it might be said

that he has made me ridiculous by his way of dealing with it.'

'You are quite right,' said Edward; 'but it would be difficult to get at him; for he has taken care to plead his cause like a true advocate as he is, in the course of his explanation, and by the manner in which he has interwoven what is depreciatory, with the professed object of exalting the subject which he put into the front of his discourse.'

'To take care to proceed like a true advocate,' said Leonard, 'is not at all bad; and why should I not take every opportunity to exercise myself in the legitimate and becoming parts of my art? Besides, I could not say no to the ladies, and they could not have provided me with anything better on which to exercise that way of thinking which I openly enough confess to. Yet, after all, I have not proceeded at all like an advocate, as I did not introduce into my speech the slightest appeal to our fair judges for favour.'

'We must also bear you witness,' said Ernest, 'that you have left out much which might have otherwise been brought forward, whether it was that you had it not in hand, or that you dropped it to spare time, and not to speak too learnedly and unintelligently before the ladies.'

'For my part,' said Ernestine, 'I should like also to praise him for having so honourably carried out his promise to keep himself as much as possible away from what we perhaps might hear to-morrow in the places of public worship.'

'Well then,' said Caroline, 'if it is not possible to bring him forthwith to trial, the first question is how to refute him; and unless I am wrong, it is your turn,

Ernest, to speak, and it stands with you to save the honour of our theme.'

'I intend,' said Ernest, 'to do the last without undertaking to do the first; and for my part, I should not care to combine these two things with each other. Besides, the refutation would draw me away to other subjects, and I might then myself become liable to a penalty. And further, to one who is not accustomed to extempore connected speaking, nothing is more difficult in doing so than to follow up the train of thought of another.'

He then proceeded as follows : ' As to what I was about to say, before you spoke, Leonard, I should not have known to make the distinction as to whether it is a commending or an extolling of the subject. But now I know that, according to your manner, I am about to extol it, for I will also eulogize the Festival of Christmas as excellent in its kind. But with regard to the laudation of it to the effect that it is good in its kind and conception, I shall not, like you, leave that out of account, but will rather proceed upon it. Only I may remark that your definition of a festival is not sufficient for me, as it was one-sided, and generally was only adapted to your own requirement. My requirement, however, is different from yours, and I must bring in the other side of the subject. You only looked at it from the point of view that every festival is a *commemoration* of something, but what concerns me most is *what* it commemorates. Accordingly, I say that a festival is founded only to recall to remembrance something of which the very idea is fitted to excite a certain mood and sentiment in the souls of men ; and the excellence of any festival consists in the fact that this result is realized in the whole range of the sphere to which it belongs, and in a vivid degree. The mood, however, which it is the object of our festival to produce, is joy ; and it is so evident that it does vividly quicken and widely spread this condition of mind, that nothing requires to be said about it, as every one sees this with his own eyes. There is only one difficulty which I might be expected to remove. For it might be said that it is not the peculiar and essential character of the festival at ✓ all that produces this effect of joy, but only what is accidental to it, such as the presents that are given and received. I must therefore proceed to show how erroneous such a view is. To me it is evidently so ; for if you give the children the same things at any other time, you will not thereby evoke even the semblance of their Christmas joy until you come to the opposite point with them, namely, that at which their own birthday festival is celebrated. I believe that I am right in calling this an opposite point, and certainly no one will deny that the enjoyment of a birthday has quite a different character from the enjoyment of Christmas. The former has all the inwardness which is produced from its being confined to a particular relation; the latter has all the fire and the quick movement of a wide-spread general feeling. Hence it appears that it is not the presents in themselves which are the cause of the joy, but presents are bestowed only because there already exists a reason for rejoicing. What is peculiar to the joy of Christmas just consists in this its great univer-sality. And this universal joy inevitably communicates, itself to the presents too, so that in a great part of Christendom, or so far as the beautiful old custom yet reaches, every one is occupied with preparing their gifts ; and in this consciousness lies a great part of the

charm with which the festival lays hold of all. Imagine
for a moment that only a single family kept up this
custom, while all the other families in the same place
had given it up, then the impression connected with it
would no longer be the same. But the fact that there
are so many taken up with it together, the zealous
working in preparation for the appointed hour of the
festival, and the Christmas markets outside open to all
and arranged for the great crowd, all glittering with
presents which with their brilliant illuminations look in
the winter night like sparkling stars gleaming upon the
earth, so that the heavens appear to reflect them back
again : all this gives to the presents their peculiar value.
And what is so universal cannot for that very reason be
considered to have been arbitrarily devised or externally
agreed upon, but must have a common internal principle
or reason; otherwise it could neither produce such an
identical effect, nor even continue to exist at all; as,
in fact, we have sufficiently seen from many modern
attempts of the kind. This internal principle, however,
can be no other than this, that the appearance of the
Redeemer is the source of all other joy in the Christian
world; and for this reason there is nothing else can
deserve to be so celebrated. For some, indeed, whom I
cannot call to mind without accusing them in the very fact
for so doing, have transferred the universal joy from this
festival to the New Year, or to that day on which the
change and contrast of time is most prominently shown.
Many in doing this have merely proceeded without
thinking, and it would be unjust to assert wherever
presents are given at the New Year instead of at
Christmas that this always indicates a lack of partici-
pation in what is specially Christian in our life. Yet

this divergence in custom is evidently not unconnected with some such putting of the Christian element in the background; and it is specially in place with those who lack inward attachment to it, and live only in the sphere of change, and who therefore make their special day of joy of that very day which is consecrated to the renewal of the perishable. For the rest of us, however, who ✓ are indeed likewise subject to the change of time, yet desire not to live in what is transitory, the birth of the Redeemer is the only universal festival of joy, because there is for us really no other principle of joy than our redemption. And in the development of this redemption the birth of the divine Child is the first bright point, and we wait for no other point of time after it, nor can we longer delay our joy. Hence, too, there is no other special festival which has such similarity with this universal one as that of baptism, by which the principle of joy in the divine is appropriated to the little ones. And I may observe that this explains the peculiar charm of that graceful narrative in which the two were presented to us in combination. Yes, Leonard, we may look at it as we may, but there is no escaping the fact. The original life and joy of nature, in which those opposi-⌐ tions between appearance and essence, time and eternity, do not yet appear, are not ours. And if we think of this as in some One, then we must also think of Him as a Redeemer; and for us He must begin as a divine Child. On the other hand, we ourselves begin with discord and division, and we only attain to harmony by redemption, which is really nothing but the removal of those opposi- tions; and for this very reason redemption can only proceed from one in the case of whom they did not require to be removed. Certain it is that no one can

E

deny that the peculiar nature of this festival is this, that
we become conscious of the inmost ground and of the
inexhaustible power of a new untroubled life, and that
in the first germ of it we at the same time behold its
fairest blossom and even its highest perfection.   However unconsciously it may exist in many, the wondrous
feeling connected with the miraculous cannot be resolved
into anything else than into this concentrated vision of a
new world.   This world lays hold of every one, and its
Originator is represented in a thousand images and in the
most diverse manner.   He is represented as the rising
and returning sun, as the spring-time of the Spirit, as
the King of a better Kingdom, as the most faithful
Ambassador of God, and as the most lovable Prince of
Peace.   And so I come at last, Leonard, to refute you,
even by agreeing with you and putting together comparatively the different views from which we started.
However insufficient the historical traces of His life
may be when the subject is critically examined in a
lower sense, yet the festival does not depend on this
condition of the case, but on the necessity of a Redeemer,
as well as on the experience of a heightened sense of
existence which can be referred to no other beginning
than the one in question.   Often you find comparatively
even less trace of the thread on which a crystallization
has had to attach itself, yet even the slightest trace suffices
to prove to you that it was there.   So likewise it has
really been Christ to whose powers of attraction this
new world has owed its formation ; and whoever—as you
yourself are inclined to do—recognises Christianity as a
present power and as the great form of the new life, he
must regard this festival as sacred, not in the fashion of
those who do not dare to impugn what is not understood,

but by completely understanding it and all its details, including the presents and the children, the night and the light.—And with this little improvement, which I hope will be pleasing to you, I repeat your challenge. And I trust, or rather prophesy, that the beautiful festival will for all time preserve the gladsome childlikeness with which it always returns to us. And to all who celebrate it I wish that true joy which is experienced in the finding again of the higher life, from which alone all its dear delights really spring.'

'I must beg your pardon, Ernest,' said Agnes. 'I had feared that I should not at all understand you; but this has not been the case, for you have very well shown that the religious element is really the essence of the festival. Only it would appear, from what has been as yet made out, as if we women should have less share in the joy, because there is less of that deviation from nature manifested in us. But I can also explain that well enough for myself.'

'Very easily,' said Leonard. 'It might just be at once said, and it is as evident as can be, that women bear everything easily as regards themselves, and strive after little enjoyment, but that as their inmost suffering is fellow-suffering, so also their joy is sympathetic joy. Only you must see how you are to keep yourself right with the authority of the sacred text which you will never give up, and which so evidently represents the women as the primary originators of the discord of nature and of all the need of redemption. But if I were Frederica, I would declare war upon Ernest in that he has so lightly, and without consideration of his own circumstances, given the preference to baptism over betrothal, which, I hope, is also to be regarded as a beautiful and joyful sacrament.'

'Don't answer him, Ernest,' said Frederica; 'he has already answered himself.'

'How so?' asked Leonard.

'Why, evidently,' replied Ernestine, 'in that you spoke of your own circumstances; but people like you never observe when you mix up your own dear selves. Ernest, however, made an excellent distinction; and he will surely say to you that that relation comes closer to the joy of a birthday than to the joy of Christmas.'

'Or,' added Ernest, 'if you will have something Christian in this connection, that it is more like Good Friday or Easter. But now, passing from what has already been presented, let us hear what Edward will say.'

Edward thereupon began to speak as follows: 'It has already been remarked on an occasion like this by one better than I, that the last are in the worst position when any subject whatever is discoursed about in this way. This is not only so from the earlier speakers taking up what might have otherwise remained to be said, as indeed you two have given yourselves little concern in this respect about me by leaving over some points in detail which I might take up. But the difficulty for me mainly lies in this, that certain echoes of every speech remain in the minds of the hearers, and that these beget an always increasing resistance which the last speaker has the greatest difficulty in overcoming. Hence I must look round for some assistance, and attach what I am about to say to something that is known and dear to you, so that it may the more easily find entrance into your thoughts. Now, as Leonard has had the more external biographers of Christ very often before his mind in trying to discover what was historical in them, I shall turn to the mystical one among the four evangelists who presents but little in the way of individual events. Indeed, we do not find in him anything of Christmas as an external fact; but in his soul there rules an eternal, childlike Christmas joy. And what he gives us, is the spiritual and higher view of our festival. As you know, he commences thus: "In the beginning was the Word, and the Word was with God, and the Word was God. ... In Him was life; and the life was the light of men. ... And the Word was made flesh, and dwelt among us; and we beheld His glory, the glory as of the only-begotten of the Father, full of grace and truth." And it is thus that I prefer to regard the object of this festival, not as a mere child fashioned and appearing so and so, and born from this woman or that, or here or there, but as the Word made flesh, the Word which was God, and was with God. The flesh, however, as we know, is nothing else than our finite, limited, sensible nature. The Word, on the other hand, is the thought or consciousness; and its becoming incarnate is therefore the appearing of this original and divine thing in that form. Accordingly what we celebrate is just what we are in ourselves as a whole; in other words, it is human nature, or whatever you may call it, contemplated and known from the divine principle. But why we must set up One in whom human nature alone can thus exhibit itself, and why we must recognise this very One, and in His case refer this oneness of the divine and the earthly specially to His birth, and not regard it as a later fruit of His life: all this will be clear from what is to follow. What is man-in-himself but the terrestrial spirit itself, or the earthly life knowing itself in its eternal being, and in its ever changing process of becoming? So far there is no corruption in man, and no fall, and no need of a redemption. When the individual, however, attaches himself to the other formations of the earth, and seeks the knowledge of himself in them (for, in fact, conscious knowledge of them dwells only in him), he is only in a condition of becoming, and is in a state of fall and corruption, or of discord and confusion; and he finds his redemption only in Man as such, Man in himself. Therein he finds in fact that very oneness of the eternal being and becoming of the spirit which can manifest itself upon this planet, and arise in every one only by every one contemplating and loving all that becomes, including himself, in the eternal Being alone. And in so far as he appears as in the process of becoming, he wills to be nothing else than a thought of the eternal Being; nor will he be grounded in any other eternal Being than in that which is one and the same with the ever changing and returning process. Hence the oneness of being and becoming thus indicated, is found eternally in humanity, because humanity is and becomes eternally as the essential Man, as Man in himself. But in the individual, this oneness, so far as it is in him, must consciously arise as his thought, and as the thought of a common doing and living in which that knowledge which is proper to our planet not only is, but also becomes. And it is only when the individual contemplates and cultivates humanity as a living fellowship of individuals, and carries its spirit and consciousness in himself, and loses and finds again his separate existence in it, that he has the higher life and the peace of God in himself. Now this fellowship by which the true essential man-in-himself is thus exhibited or restored, constitutes the Church. The Church is therefore related to all else that becomes human around it and out of it, as the self-consciousness of the humanity in the individuals is related to what is unconscious. Every one then in whom this self-consciousness arises comes into the Church. Hence no one who is not himself really in the Church can truly and livingly have science in himself; and, on the other hand, such a one can repudiate or deny the Church only outwardly and not inwardly. But there may well be those in the Church who cannot be said to have science in themselves; for they may possess that higher self-consciousness in the form of feeling, although not also in cognition. This is just the case with women; and it is at the same time the very reason why they attach themselves so much more fervently and exclusively to the Church. Now this fellowship as a process of becoming, is likewise a thing that has arisen and become; and as a fellowship of individuals, it has arisen and become by communication of that fellowship. We must therefore seek a starting-point for this communication, although we know that it must start again self-actively from every individual in order that the man - in - himself, or what is essentially human, may thus be brought forth and take shape in every individual. But the first fellowship of feeling which broke out freely and self-actively on the day of Pentecost may, as it were, be called the birth of the Church, and He who is regarded as the primary point in the beginning of the Church, or as its conception and inception, must be already born as the Man-in-himself, or as the God-man; He must carry the self-cognition of humanity in Himself, and be the Light of men from the beginning. For we, indeed, are born again through the Spirit of the Church. But the Spirit Itself only goes out from the Son, who requires no new birth, but is born originally from God. Thus He is the Son of Man absolutely. All that was before Him was a pre-figuration of Him, and was related to Him; and only through this relation was it good and divine. Yet in Him we celebrate not only ourselves but all who will yet come, as well as all who have ever been; for they were only anything in so far as He was in them and they in Him. In Christ, then, we see the Spirit, according to the kind and manner of our earth, primordially take the form of self-consciousness in the individual. The Father and the Brethren dwell equably in Him, and are one in Him; devotion and love are His very being. Therefore every mother who feels that she has borne a man, and who knows by a heavenly annunciation that the Spirit of the Church, the Holy Ghost, lives in her, forthwith presents her child on that account with all her heart to the Church, and she claims to be allowed to do this as a right; and such a mother sees Christ also in her child, and this is just the inexpressible mother-feeling which compensates for all else. And in like manner, every one of us beholds his own higher birth in the Birth of Christ; and in such a one there thereby lives nothing but devotion and love, and in him too does the eternal Son of God appear. Hence it is that this festival breaks forth like a heavenly light shining out of the night. Therefore is it that there is a universal pulsating of joy in the whole new-born world, which only those members of the race that have been long sick or maimed do not feel. And this is the very glory of the festival which it was your wish to hear lauded also by me.—But as I see, I am not to be the last after all; for our long expected friend is now indeed also here.'

Joseph, in fact, had come in during this discourse, and

although he had entered and sat down quietly, Edward had observed him. 'By no means,' said he, when Edward thus addressed him, 'for you shall certainly be the last. I have not come to deliver a discourse, but to make myself glad with you; and if I may honestly say it, it appears to me somewhat strange and almost foolish that you should be going on thus, however fine it may in other respects have been. But I already observe that your evil principle is again among you,—this Leonard, the thinking, reflecting, dialectical, over-intellectual man, against whom you have probably been directing your discourse. For assuredly it cannot have been needed for yourself, and you would not have otherwise fallen on the idea; and to him, after all, it could be of no avail. And the poor ladies have also had to fall in with it perforce. Only think what beautiful melodies they would have sung to you, with all the piety of your discourses dwelling in them far more inwardly; or how charmingly, from hearts full of love and joy, they might have chatted with you, saying what would have otherwise pleased and enlivened you in a better way than they can have been by these solemn speeches of yours! For my part, I cannot to-day take up with such things at all. To me all forms have become too stiff, and all discoursing too tedious and cold. The unspeakable subject demands and even produces in me an unspeakable joy; in my gladness I can only exult and shout for joy like a child. To me to-day all men are children; and for that very reason they are only the dearer to me. The solemn wrinkles are for once smoothed away; years and cares do not stand written on the brow; the eye sparkles and lives again; and in them all is the presentiment of a beautiful and gracious existence. To my own delight I have also myself become wholly a child. As a child quenches his childish pain, and suppresses his sighs, and draws in his tears when a childish joy is communicated to him, so to me to-day the long, deep, imperishable pain of life is soothed as never before. I feel myself at home, and as it were new born in the better world, in which pain and sorrow have no more a meaning, nor a place. With glad eye I look upon everything, even upon what wounds us deeply. As Christ had no bride but the Church, no children but His friends, no home but the temple and the world, and yet His heart was full of heavenly love and joy, so do I seem to myself to be also born to strive after things like these. Thus have I roamed around the whole evening, taking everywhere the heartiest interest in all the trifles and amusements I have seen ; and I have loved and laughed, and enjoyed it all. It has been one long loving kiss which I have given to the world ; and now my enjoyment with you is to be the last impress of the lip. For you know well that to me you are the dearest of all. Come, then, and bring the child above all things, if she is not yet asleep ; and let me see your glories ; and let us be glad, and sing something pious and joyous.'

APPENDIX.

—o—

DR. CARL SCHWARZ ON SCHLEIERMACHER'S *CHRISTMAS EVE*.

SCHLEIERMACHER's *Christmas Eve* was written five years later than his *Monologues*. He had now fought through the pain felt on account of Eleonore. This storm did not break him, but rather confirmed his moral energy. His real and deep religiousness and the power of his moral will, carried him safely through that severe conflict. He found reviving and healing influence in his friendships, and especially in the sympathy of noble and spiritually cultivated women, to whom he opened his soul. The *Christmas Eve* introduces us into this circle, and it closes the period of pain like a reconciling harmony. This work, like the *Monologues*, was completed in a few weeks as if by a touch of inspiration; and on the evening of Christmas 1805, the last of the manuscript was given to the printer. The whole arrangement of the composition is artistic, and yet it is as simple as it is graceful. It recalls the Dialogues of Plato, with which Schleiermacher at that time was much occupied; and it reflects the manner in which these Dialogues present their earnest and instructive matter graced and enlivened by a social circle of living personalities. So we have here a kind of Christian 'Symposion' around the Christmas table, representing a circle of highly cultivated men and women so combined as to adorn the solemn festival with fair blossoms, and to blend into a beautiful harmony a rich variety of different moods and views.

The women introduce the whole in a charming way, and they form, as it were, the accompanying music of the movement. They exhibit the element of deep inward religiousness that is elevated above all theology, and they are shown reconciling and harmonizing all sharp tones and dissonances. Music is spoken of frequently and at some length; and the Dialogue is repeatedly broken by it coming in. The thought is expressed and dwelt upon, that music has the closest affinity with the religious feeling, and that Christianity and music must go together, because they mutually elucidate and elevate each other. The child Sophie exhibits religion in its most original form, as breaking forth directly from the depths of the soul, and as still entirely merged in the musical spirit. The objection first suggested by Henriette Herz, the talented friend of Schleiermacher, has been frequently put forward, that the sketch of the child is a failure, and that she makes throughout the impression of being wise beyond her years, or of being precocious and old-fashioned. We cannot agree with this view, for with all the peculiarity and deep thoughtfulness of her sayings, and with all the romanticism thrown into her dark, expressive eyes, we hold that the charm of originality and unconsciousness is not wanting in her. The conversation proceeds about various matters, which, however, are always connected with the Christmas festival and Christmas feelings, and returns to them again. Remarks are made about what real joy is, about the high significance of art, and especially of sacred music, about the true character of childhood and what constitutes it, as well as about the distinguishing characteristics of the different nature of men and women. The Dialogue is thus carried on, often with witty and argumentative digressions and retorts, as was so characteristic of Schleiermacher, but yet always in such a way that the warm heart everywhere thrills through, and so that the fine aroma of a truly cultured society is felt to permeate everything. The women begin with narratives about past Christmas festivals and the feelings then experienced. Each of them proceeds to give a contribution of her own, a little picture set into the frame of the beautiful festival. When they have ended, the men declare themselves also ready to give each his contribution to the banquet, as a return gift in the English or Greek fashion, and this is done by each of them making a discourse on the theme of the day, the sacred festival of Christmas.

The speeches which thus follow, form the kernel of the whole production ; and they contain in germ, and in the most graceful and accessible form, the fundamental thoughts of Schleiermacher's Christology, and even of his whole Theology.) The various sides of Schleiermacher's nature, and the spiritual tendencies which so wonderfully met in him, are assigned to the several speakers. The opposite representations which here seem to be in conflict, are in truth complementary to each other. It is not a mere historical conjunction of the divergent theological parties of that time that Schleiermacher proceeds to give us; rather it is the different sides of his own theology which are only apparently separated, but are again united at the centre. It is Schleiermacher himself who appears) in Protean transformations under the successive names. It is but one light that is here broken up into different colours.

And, in the first place, we have Leonard, 'the unbelieving knave,' as he is called in jest by his friends, the 'thinking, reflective, dialectical, over-intellectual man.' This figure is sketched with particular fondness. It is Leonard who always adds the salt to the conversation, and who elevates the tone of it when it sometimes becomes too soft and lyrical, by lifting it up into the sphere of the understanding. He is not a mere cold advocate of enlightenment and a rationalist in the style of his time. He is rather to be regarded as the representative of the sceptico-critical spirit which was so powerful in Schleiermacher, and which belonged so inseparably to his nature ; the beneficial, health-preserving salt which was so happily associated and mingled with his mystical tendency. Leonard applies his criticism mainly to the historical representations of the birth of Christ as they have been handed down to us by

the first three evangelists, the so-called synoptists; and this
criticism, it is well known, Schleiermacher never recalled nor
minimized, but in this connection he always remained a
rationalist. He carried on the critical investigations regarding
the origin of the writings of the New Testament and their
unhistorical elements, and did so with more pointedness
and with the utmost boldness, especially in connection with
the miraculous narratives. These investigations had been
begun by the rationalists. Leonard comes to the result that
the historical basis of the life of Jesus is generally very
uncertain and contradictory, and that it is open to the conflict
of parties, and especially that the narratives of the birth of
Jesus suffer from these contradictions and incredibilities.
And hence he infers that the synoptical narratives have not
founded the Festival of Christmas ; but rather conversely, that
this festival with its suggestive customs has become the ground
of the faith that is maintained in common, as it so often
happens in fact, that the customs of a following age become
the means of forming anew and confirming the preceding
history. He seeks the significance of the Festival of Christmas,
not so much in its ecclesiastical as in its genuinely human
relation, in its being the Christmas of the *household* and of
the *children ;* and he will therefore interpret everything sym-
bolically — the Child, the night, the lights, and so on — as
presenting beautiful images of the spiritual life and of man's
being born again.

Ernest, on the other hand, brings specially forward the
religious side of the festival. He starts from *the religious feeling
and the need of the community,* and he develops from this point
of view the significance of the Redeemer and of the redemption. As is well known, this is the very centre of Schleiermacher's Christology ; and, although it is as yet stated only in
a simple form, this representation is of special interest to us
as regards the construction of Schleiermacher's view of Christ,
and more particularly in reference to His uniqueness and sinlessness, as represented in his later dogmatic system. We are

able to recognise these elements of his doctrine here in all their main features, as a postulate of the religious feeling. The birth of the Redeemer is the universal festival of joy, because there is really no other principle of joy than the redemption; and in the development of redemption the birth of Christ is the first clear point in history. Hence it was necessary that the Redeemer should begin as a divine Child in unity with God, whereas we begin with discordance and division. And hence He was already at birth what we only become by regeneration; and thus the special significance of the Christmas Festival consists in this, *that we do become conscious of the inexhaustible power of a new undisturbed life.* This apparent refutation of the scepticism of Leonard is, however, in truth an acceptance and completion of it, as Ernest himself puts it in the words: 'However insufficient the historical traces of His life may be when the subject is critically examined in a lower sense, yet the Festival does not depend on this condition of the case, but on the necessity of a Redeemer, as well as on the experience of a heightened sense of existence which can be referred to no other beginning than the one in question.'

While Leonard thus represents *historical criticism*, and Ernest *religious feeling* with its necessary return to the beginnings of Christianity, Edward is the representative of the *speculative element* in Schleiermacher. His preference for the Gospel of John and for that speculation which finds a point of attachment in it, is here expressed. As distinguished from Leonard, Edward will keep to the Fourth Evangelist and to the tender ideal Gospel, in which there is in general little in the way of external and individual facts communicated, and there is no history of the Nativity at all. To him the object of the Festival is not so much the Child as the Word become flesh; it is ourselves we celebrate, that is to say, human nature regarded from the divine principle. For Christ is nothing else than Man in himself, the eternal Being in the process of change and becoming, the unity of the divine and the earthly. This unity is in us too, but only in the form of individuality, of becoming; and it is the task of every individual to elevate himself into human nature, into eternal Being. This is done through the fellowship of the Christian Church, which is at once in process of becoming and is become; and as such it goes back to the point from which the communication of divine being proceeded, to the *Man* in himself, or the Son of man absolutely. To Him everything in the history of humanity is related. All that came before pointed forward to Him, and all that has followed points back to Him. This speculative view of Christ is evidently closely connected with the religious view of His person; and in the development of Schleiermacher's dogmatic theology, we find a fundamental metaphysical principle as the ultimate basis of the religious postulate of the uniqueness and sinlessness of Jesus : it is the unity of the ideal and the historical, a consciousness of God of such strength and powerfulness that it was at the same time *a being of God in Christ.*

Lastly, at the close of the whole Dialogue, Joseph comes forward, having entered quietly during the last speech. He is the representative of the *mystical element* in all its inward fervour and unbrokenness ; he represents, as it were, the Moravianism that remained in Schleiermacher. To him all this discoursing appears foolish. For him all forms are too stiff, all words wearisome and cold. The unspeakable subject demands an unspeakable joy. He will become wholly a child, and only laugh and shout for joy like a child. The religious feeling, in a manner very characteristic of Schleiermacher, thus breaks powerfully and overwhelmingly through all the barriers of artificial reflection thrown up to oppose it like a stream of holy music, and in this music all is resolved. 'Come, then,' it is said in conclusion, 'and let us be glad, and sing something pious and joyous.'

MORRISON AND GIBB, PRINTERS, EDINBURGH.

A NEW AND CHEAPER EDITION.

Just published, in crown 8vo, price 3s. 6d.,

BEYOND THE STARS;

OR,

𝔥𝔢𝔞𝔳𝔢𝔫, 𝔦𝔱𝔰 𝔦𝔫𝔥𝔞𝔟𝔦𝔱𝔞𝔫𝔱𝔰, 𝔬𝔠𝔠𝔲𝔭𝔞𝔱𝔦𝔬𝔫𝔰, 𝔞𝔫𝔡 𝔩𝔦𝔣𝔢.

BY THOMAS HAMILTON, D.D.,

PRESIDENT OF QUEEN'S COLLEGE, BELFAST;
AUTHOR OF 'HISTORY OF THE IRISH PRESBYTERIAN CHURCH,' ETC. ETC.

PRESS NOTICES OF THE FIRST EDITION.

' A good book upon a grand subject. . . . His writing is solid, he dissipates dreams, but he establishes authorized hopes. . . . This is a book which a believer will enjoy all the more when he draws nearer to those blessed fields " beyond the stars."'—Mr. SPURGEON in *Sword and Trowel.*

' The work of a man of strong sense and great power of lucid thought and expression, one who has deep springs of tenderness. He puts himself well in touch with his audience, and arranges what he has to say in the clearest manner.'—*British Weekly.*

' The author's natural and sympathetic eloquence lends at times a brightness, and again a more pathetic charm to his theme. We cannot doubt that his book will comfort as well as interest a wide circle of readers.'—*Scottish Leader.*

' Many a bruised heart will be made joyful on reading this book. . . . On a former occasion, when reviewing a book by the same author, we congratulated the Irish Presbyterian Church on having among her younger ministers a writer of such promise and power. We believe we may now congratulate the wider Christian Church on a teacher and guide whose words will fortify and cheer wherever the English language is spoken.'—*Presbyterian Messenger.*

' There is not a dry or uninteresting page in it, and most of the chapters are profoundly absorbing in their style and matter. It reads like a novel, yet there is nothing mawkish or sentimental about it; but it is reverent, devout, frank, manly, and orthodox in its tone and character.'—*Christian Advocate.*

' The tone is reverent, the style is clear, the reasoning is careful. Its capital type will recommend it to the weary sight of some to whom the " land of distances " is no longer the land that is very far off.'—*Church Bells.*

' Dr. Hamilton endeavours to tell in plain and popular language all that the Bible reveals about the other life. The tone of the book is admirable ; devout and modest throughout.'—*London Quarterly Review.*

WORKS BY PROF. FRANZ DELITZSCH, D.D.

Just published, in 2 Vols., demy 8vo, price 21s.,

A NEW COMMENTARY ON GENESIS.

"Thirty-five years have elapsed since Prof. Delitzsch's Commentary on Genesis first appeared; fifteen years since the fourth edition was published in 1872. Ever in the van of historical and philological research, the venerable author now comes forward with another fresh edition, in which he incorporates what fifteen years have achieved for illustration and criticism of the text of Genesis. . . . We congratulate Prof. Delitzsch on this new edition. By it, not less than by his other Commentaries, he has earned the gratitude of every lover of Biblical science, and we shall be surprised if, in the future, many do not acknowledge that they have found in it a welcome help and guide.'—Professor S. R. DRIVER in *The Academy*.

'Marked, like all others of the author's writings, by an undercurrent of deep spirituality, which again and again comes to the surface in a full wave of enthusiastic utterance.'—*Record*.

'By far the most learned Commentary on Genesis existing in the English, and probably in any, language.'—*Rock*.

'The work of a reverent mind and a sincere believer; and not seldom there are touches of great beauty and of deep spiritual insight in it. The learning, it is needless to say, is very wide and comprehensive.'—*Guardian*.

In crown 8vo, price 4s. 6d.,

OLD TESTAMENT HISTORY OF REDEMPTION.

'Few who will take the trouble to look into it will not readily acknowledge that it is not only a masterly work, such as few men, if any, besides the Leipzig professor could give, but that there is nothing to be compared with it as a handbook for students."—*Literary World*.

In One Volume, 8vo, price 12s.,

A SYSTEM OF BIBLICAL PSYCHOLOGY.

'This admirable volume ought to be carefully read by every thinking clergyman.'—*Literary Churchman*.

'An excellent work, clearly written, full of thought, rich in illustration, and giving a most accurate view of the different parts which constitute our nature.'—*Churchman*.

In Two Volumes, 8vo, price 21s.,

COMMENTARY ON THE EPISTLE TO THE HEBREWS.

KEIL AND DELITZSCH'S
COMMENTARIES ON, AND INTRODUCTION TO, THE OLD TESTAMENT.

This Series (published in Clark's Foreign Theological Library) is now completed in Twenty-seven Volumes, price £7, 2s. nett. Any Eight Volumes are now supplied for £2, 2s., or more at same ratio.

Separate Volumes may be had, price 10s. 6d. each.

'Very high merit for thorough Hebrew scholarship, and for keen critical sagacity, belongs to these Old Testament Commentaries. No scholar will willingly dispense with them.'—*British Quarterly Review*.

NEW WORK BY PROFESSOR DELITZSCH.

Just published, in post 8vo, price 6s.,

IRIS:

Studies in Colour and Talks about Flowers.

By PROFESSOR FRANZ DELITZSCH, D.D.

TRANSLATED BY REV. ALEXANDER CUSIN, M.A., EDINBURGH.

CONTENTS:—CHAP. I. The Blue of the Sky.—II. Black and White.—
III. Purple and Scarlet.—IV. Academic Official Robes and their Colours.
—V. The Talmud and Colours.—VI. Gossip about Flowers and their
Perfume.—VII. A Doubtful Nosegay.—VIII. The Flower-Riddle of the
Queen of Sheba.—IX. The Bible and Wine.—X. Dancing and Criticism
of the Pentateuch as mutually related.—XI. Love and Beauty.—XII.
Eternal Life: Eternal Youth.

EXTRACT FROM THE PREFACE.

'The subjects of the following papers are old pet children, which have
grown up with me ever since I began to feel and think. . . . I have collected
them here under the emblematical name of Iris. The prismatic colours of
the rainbow, the brilliant sword-lily, that wonderful part of the eye which
gives to it its colour, and the messenger of heaven who beams with joy,
youth, beauty, and love, are all named Iris. The varied contents of my book
stand related on all sides to that wealth of ideas which are united in this
name.'—FRANZ DELITZSCH.

' A series of delightful lectures. . . . The pages sparkle with a gem-like
light. The thoughts on the varied subjects touched upon fascinate and
interest; their mode of expression is full of beauty.'—*Scotsman.*

Now ready, SECOND EDITION, crown 8vo, price 6s.,

THE LORD'S PRAYER:

A Practical Meditation.

By REV. NEWMAN HALL, LL.D.

CRITICAL NOTICES OF THE FIRST EDITION.

'Its devotional element is robust and practical. The thought is not thin,
and the style is clear. Thoroughly readable; enriched by quotations and
telling illustrations.'—*The Churchman.*

Dr. THEODORE CUYLER, of Brooklyn, writes:—' His keen and discriminating
spiritual insight insures great accuracy, and imparts a priceless value to the
work. . . . It is the very book to assist ministers of the gospel in the study
of the Model Prayer; it is equally stimulating and quickening to private
Christians in their quiet hours of meditation and devotion.'

Mr. C. H. SPURGEON writes:—' Evangelical and practical through and
through. . . . Many sparkling images and impressive passages adorn the
pages; but everywhere practical usefulness has been pursued.'

Dr. REYNOLDS, President of Cheshunt College, writes:—' Not only range
but also depth of research. Some of the deepest questions of philosophical
theology are discussed with keen insight and admirable temper. Much
thought is compressed into small space, and even into few words, which burn
oftentimes with white heat.'

' The author's well-known catholicity, evangelical fervour, and firm
adherence to evangelical principles, are conspicuous features of this really
stimulating and suggestive exposition. An amount of freshness which is
wonderful.'—*Christian.*

WORKS BY PROFESSOR A. B. BRUCE, D.D.

In demy 8vo, Fourth Edition, price 10s. 6d.,

THE TRAINING OF THE TWELVE;
OR,

EXPOSITION OF PASSAGES IN THE GOSPELS EXHIBITING THE TWELVE DISCIPLES OF JESUS UNDER DISCIPLINE FOR THE APOSTLESHIP.

BY A. B. BRUCE, D.D.,
PROFESSOR OF DIVINITY, FREE CHURCH COLLEGE, GLASGOW.

'Here we have a really great book on an important, large, and attractive subject—a book full of loving, wholesome, profound thoughts about the fundamentals of Christian faith and practice.'—*British and Foreign Evangelical Review.*

'It is some five or six years since this work first made its appearance, and now that a second edition has been called for, the author has taken the opportunity to make some alterations which are likely to render it still more acceptable. Substantially, however, the book remains the same, and the hearty commendation with which we noted its first issue applies to it at least as much now.'—*Rock.*

'A great book, full of suggestion and savour. It should be the companion of the minister, for the theme is peculiarly related to himself, and he would find it a very pleasant and profitable companion, for its author has filled it with good matter.'—Mr. SPURGEON in *Sword and Trowel.*

'A more wise, scholarly, and more helpful book has not been published for many years past.'—*Wesleyan Methodist Magazine.*

BY THE SAME AUTHOR.

In demy 8vo, Third Edition, price 10s. 6d.,

THE HUMILIATION OF CHRIST,
IN ITS PHYSICAL, ETHICAL, AND OFFICIAL ASPECTS.

SIXTH SERIES OF CUNNINGHAM LECTURES.

'These lectures are able and deep-reaching to a degree not often found in the religious literature of the day; withal, they are fresh and suggestive. . . . The learning and the deep and sweet spirituality of this discussion will commend it to many faithful students of the truth as it is in Jesus.'—*Congregationalist.*

'We have not for a long time met with a work so fresh and suggestive as this of Professor Bruce. . . . We do not know where to look at our English Universities for a treatise so calm, logical, and scholarly.'—*English Independent.*

'The title of the book gives but a faint conception of the value and wealth of its contents. . . . Dr. Bruce's work is really one of exceptional value; and no one can read it without perceptible gain in theological knowledge.'—*English Churchman.*

NEW WORK BY PROFESSOR A. B. BRUCE, D.D.

Just published, in post 8vo, price 7s. 6d.,

THE KINGDOM OF GOD;

OR, CHRIST'S TEACHING ACCORDING TO THE SYNOPTICAL GOSPELS.

By A. B. BRUCE, D.D.,

**PROFESSOR OF NEW TESTAMENT EXEGESIS IN THE
FREE CHURCH COLLEGE, GLASGOW.**

CONTENTS:—Critical Introduction.—CHAP. I. Christ's Idea of the King-dom.—II. Christ's Attitude towards the Mosaic Laws.—III. The Conditions of Entrance.—IV. Christ's Doctrine of God.—V. Christ's Doctrine of Man.—VI. The Relation of Jesus to Messianic Hopes and Functions.—VII. The Son of Man and the Son of God.—VIII. The Righteousness of the Kingdom—Negative Aspect.—IX. The Right-eousness of the Kingdom—Positive Aspect.—X. The Death of Jesus and its Significance.—XI. The Kingdom and the Church.—XII. The Parousia and the Christian Era.—XIII. The History of the Kingdom in Outline.—XIV. The End.—XV. The Christianity of Christ.—Index.

Just published, SECOND EDITION, crown 8vo, price 6s. (Revised throughout),

STUDIES IN THE CHRISTIAN EVIDENCES.

By REV. ALEXANDER MAIR, D.D.

PRESS NOTICES OF THE FIRST EDITION.

' Dr. Mair has made an honest study of Strauss, Renan, Keim, and "Super-natural Religion," and his book is an excellent one to put into the hands of doubters and inquirers.'—*English Churchman.*

'Will in every way meet the wants of the class for whom it is intended, many of whom are "wayworn and sad," amid the muddled speculations of the current day.'—*Ecclesiastical Gazette.*

'This book ought to become immensely popular. . . . That one chapter on " The Unique Personality of Christ" is a masterpiece of eloquent writing, though it is scarcely fair to mention one portion where every part is excellent. The beauties of the volume are everywhere apparent, and therefore will again attract the mind that has been once delighted with the literary feast. —*The Rock.*

' An admirable popular introduction to the study of the evidences. . . . Dr. Mair has made each line of evidence his own, and the result is a distinctly fresh and living book. The style is robust and manly; the treat-·ment of antagonists is eminently fair; and we discern throughout a soldierly straightness of aim.'—*The Baptist.*

Just published, in crown 8vo, price 6s. 6d.,

THE WAY,
THE NATURE, AND MEANS OF
REVELATION.

BY

JOHN F. WEIR, M.A.,
DEAN OF THE DEPARTMENT OF FINE ARTS, YALE UNIVERSITY.

CONTENTS:—CHAP. I. The Beginning and the Ending.—II. The Seers and Prophets.—III. The Old Testament in the Light of the New.—IV. The Son of Man.—V. The Risen Christ.—VI. The Holy Ghost.—VII. Manifestations of the Holy Ghost.—VIII. The Spirit of Truth.

A NEW 'LIFE OF JONATHAN EDWARDS.'

Just published, in fcap. 8vo, price 5s.,

JONATHAN EDWARDS.

BY

PROFESSOR ALEX. V. G. ALLEN, D.D.,
CAMBRIDGE, MASS.

EXTRACT FROM THE PREFACE.

'I have endeavoured to reproduce Edwards from his books, making his treatises, in their chronological order, contribute to his portraiture as a man and as a theologian, a task which has not been hitherto attempted. I have thought that something more than a mere recountal of facts was demanded in order to justify the endeavour to rewrite his life. What we most desire to know is, what he thought and how he came to think as he did.'

First Period.—The Parish Minister, 1703-1735.
Second Period.—The great Awakening, 1735-1750.
Third Period.—The Philosophical Theologian.

HERZOG'S ENCYCLOPÆDIA.

Now Complete, in Three Volumes, imperial 8vo, price 24s. each

ENCYCLOPÆDIA

OR

DICTIONARY

OF

BIBLICAL, HISTORICAL, DOCTRINAL, AND PRACTICAL THEOLOGY.

Based on the Real-Encyklopädie of Herzog, Plitt, and Hauck.

EDITED BY

Professor PHILIP SCHAFF, D.D., LL.D.,
UNION THEOLOGICAL SEMINARY, NEW YORK.

It is certain that this Encyclopædia will fill a place in our theological literature, in which, for a long time, it will have no rival.'—Prof. HODGE, *Princeton.*

' This Encyclopædia is exceedingly well done. . . . We hope that this new enterprise will be successful, and that no minister's library will long remain without a copy of this work. . . To people in the country, far from libraries, who cannot lay their hands on books, a work of this kind would simply be invaluable.'—*Daily Review.*

' We have been delighted with its comprehensiveness. We have never failed to find what we wanted.'—*Edinburgh Courant.*

'As a comprehensive work of reference, within a moderate compass, we know nothing at all equal to it in the large department which it deals with.'—*Church Bells.*

' The work will remain as a wonderful monument of industry, learning, and skill. It will be indispensable to the student of specifically Protestant theology ; nor, indeed, do we think that any scholar, whatever be his especial line of thought or study, would find it superfluous on his shelves.'—*Literary Churchman.*

' We commend this work with a touch of enthusiasm, for we have often wanted such ourselves. It embraces in its range of writers all the leading authors of Europe on ecclesiastical questions. A student may deny himself many other volumes to secure this, for it is certain to take a prominent and permanent place in our literature.'—*Evangelical Magazine.*